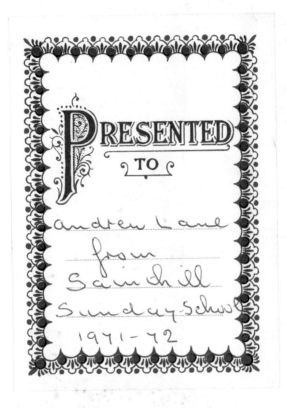

PRESENTED
TO

andrew Lane
from
Sainthill
Sunday School
1971 - 72

CATLINS COVE

CATLINS COVE

by

KIM SIMMONS

VICTORY PRESS
LONDON and EASTBOURNE

Printed in Great Britain for
VICTORY PRESS (Evangelical Publishers Ltd.),
Lottbridge Drove, Eastbourne, Sussex,
by Richard Clay (The Chaucer Press), Ltd.,
Bungay, Suffolk.

CHAPTER ONE

THE START OF A VENTURE

Angus watched from the train window for his first glimpse of the sea.

He had been on that journey once before with Father and Mother, but that was long ago.

Now he was going home, to a new home, with Uncle Roger, Aunt Anthea, Alex and Penny and Paul. He would have to stay there till his parents came back from abroad.

"How many more stops is it now?" he wondered. He glanced across at an older boy sitting opposite him, deeply absorbed, with books strewn around him on the seat. He was scribbling fast in an exercise book, and Angus thought, with sympathy, "Poor wretch—he's probably swotting for some exam."

Just then the train began to slow down and Angus looked out again eagerly. "Exworth Junction!" he said aloud.

The boy opposite jumped as though he had been shot. "Exworth!" he exclaimed. "I ought to have got out at the last stop!" Scrabbling up his papers he snatched a bag from the rack above him, swung the door open and slammed it after him.

He had almost disappeared down the platform when Angus noticed that one book still lay on the seat.

He tried to get the window down, but the train

was already moving, and by the time he leaned out to shout the boy had vanished.

Angus sat down again and for the first time that day he felt a little lonely.

John, his elder brother, had been coming with him to see him settled at Catlins Cove after their parents had said goodbye.

But John had come to grief in a rugger match and would be out of action till he went back to college, so Angus was travelling alone.

At first he had been rather pleased about it, but now he was tired and hungry and a bit bothered lest he should get out at the wrong station like the other boy had done.

He crossed over to the opposite seat and picked up the book to see what the stranger was studying. To his surprise it was not a school book at all.

'The Wayfarer's Club', he read and turned the pages eagerly, finding photographs and drawings of tents, canoes, pony-trekking and every kind of outdoor sport.

The first few pages told an exciting story of the beginning of a boys' club, and Angus became so absorbed that he only realized just in time that the train was slowing down again.

Looking out he caught sight of the signboard saying Dadingford, which was the nearest point by rail to Catlins Cove.

He stuffed the paperback into his mackintosh pocket and reached for his suitcase as the train jolted to a halt.

There they were. He could see Alex and Penny, and beyond the railings was Uncle Roger's battered old car in the station yard. His new life had begun.

The long drive from the railway was super, Angus thought. After years of living in a town the farms and woods seemed like another world.

Uncle Roger's old farmhouse lay in a sheltering fold of the downs, with a fine thatched barn close by.

There was a warm welcome from his aunt, and a massive high tea awaited him in the great flag-stoned kitchen. A spaniel with five fat puppies rose to greet him. Angus knelt down and was engulfed by dogs.

He looked up at his cousins, suddenly losing his shyness. "It's going to be wizard living here!" he said.

"It's going to be fun being four of us," Penny agreed; "two boys and two girls is better than just three. We'll take you down to the shore tonight before it gets dark."

"Then hurry up and eat," urged Aunt Anthea, coming in with the teapot. "The tide will be right up in half an hour, and it will be dark before seven."

They did hurry, and were out in the lane before the evening sun left the ridge of the downs. Bess, the spaniel, forsook her puppies and came with them, and Paul ran on ahead showing off his prowess at kicking stones.

At eight years old Paul was the youngest of the four, and Angus wished he had been two years older to match himself with Penny.

Alex was twelve, nearly thirteen, and he wondered if she would be bossy, but so far she had shown no sign of it.

Catlins Cove was very small. There were three

cottages belonging to the farm tucked away up a grass track, and a little post office and general store at the cross-roads where the bus stopped.

Down at the cove itself stood several fishermen's cottages, and some old black boathouses were built almost on the shingle. Apart from these scattered buildings there was just one thatched cottage standing at the turn of the lane.

"Isn't that a little peach of a place?" said Penny, pointing it out to Angus as they went by. "I always think it's like something out of a fairytale."

"It's old Mr Broddie's cottage," Alex told him. "He owns a boathouse or two down at the cove as well."

"And the little gift kiosk that sells tea, and ices, and kites and things," added Penny. "It's all shuttered up now; they just open it in the summer when there are lots of visitors."

Angus was surprised. "Are there lots of visitors?" he exclaimed. "I never expected boats down here either!"

"There are more in the summer," said Paul, coming back to join them, and the girls told him eagerly about special friends who came with their caravan every year.

"They're Mr and Mrs Fortescue," explained Alex. "He's an antique dealer and their caravan is fab—it's quite gay here—you wait and see!"

It looked pretty enough even then. The tide was nearly full and the gulls perched like statues on the breakwaters.

Looking up, Angus saw the ruins of Catlins Castle on the cliff top, grim and gaunt against the sky.

"Why!" he cried, "that's what Dad told me about—don't they call it the Dragon Tower?"

"They do, but I don't know why," answered Alex, as she aimed a pebble at the lazy little waves that sighed up the shingle.

Penny shivered. "It's getting jolly cold," she said. "Come out of the water, Bess, you silly dog —it isn't summer yet!"

"I'm cold too," agreed Angus. "I'll race you home!"

That evening Angus had a lot of unpacking to do, for his mother had sent a big box of his clothes and books by rail the week before and, with the contents of his suitcase as well, there were things strewn all over the long, narrow room he was to share with Paul.

His cousins drifted in one by one to see how he was getting on.

Penny sorted through his little store of books, because anything in print was a delight to her.

"I say!" she exclaimed, "you've got a super thing about camping here!"

Angus dumped his school shirts on the bed, hoping that Alex would continue putting his things tidily in drawers.

"Oh, that!" he said. "It was left in the train; I haven't really read it yet, but it's about a smashing boys' club in the beginning."

"I wish we could have a club," said Paul, who was sitting on his bed nursing one of Bess's puppies. He wasn't very sure what a club was, but it sounded exciting.

Alex put the last of the pullovers and handker-

chiefs away tidily and came to look at the book as
well.

"This place is so tiny," she said, "that there isn't
anything to do except swimming and games we
make up for ourselves."

Angus joined Paul on the bed, and the puppy
crawled across onto his knees.

"It would be jolly good to have a club of our
own," he cried, "but how do they get started?"

Nobody really knew, but Alex supposed that at
first people were asked to join and then they
thought about things to do.

"Let's think about all the children that live near
enough to come here," suggested Penny, who was
very taken with the idea. "It's no good anyone
having to come by bus; the little bus only comes
twice a day. That's why we can't join anything in
Wandford although we go to school there," she explained to Angus.

"Are there any boys in the fishermen's cottages?"
asked Angus, eagerly.

Penny considered.

"There's two near this farm, Susan at the post
office and three girls and a boy down at the cove,"
she said.

"That's ten with us—no—eleven," cried Angus.

"Then there's Vivian—Versatile Vivian," remembered Alex, "but I imagine she'd think the
idea was beneath her dignity!"

Penny nodded. "But we've forgotten those two,
Bob and Betty, in the bungalow across the field.
Why don't we go and ask them all what they think
about it. They might be as keen as we are!"

"We'll go tomorrow!" cried Alex. "It's Sunday,

so they'll all be at church or at home!"

From down below she heard her mother calling. "It's cocoa time before bed," she told Angus, and picked up the sleepy puppy from his lap. "Come, my precious," she murmured into its silky ear. "Bess will be looking for you everywhere."

Church-going for the people of Catlins Cove meant a long walk over the fields to the beautiful old church in the next hamlet, or quite a long drive round by the road.

It was simply glorious, Angus thought, tramping across the meadows the next day. "Isn't it a pity Bess can't come too?" he said, and then he stopped in his tracks. "Lambs! The first I've seen this year —do wait a minute and let me watch them!"

"We'll be late for church," warned Alex, balancing on the top of a stile. Then she jumped down, saying, "Goody! I can see something too—there's Bob and Betty coming along by their hedge; if we run to the next stile we'll meet them."

Angus thought he had never seen a brother and sister more unlike each other, when the six children met on the field path.

Betty was plump and fair, and Bob, who was only Paul's age, was dark and positively skinny. But different though they might be, they were both delighted at the idea of having a club at the cove.

"I saw a whole lot of boys camping here last year," said Bob, gleefully. "They cooked sausages and had a camp fire! When can we begin, Alex?"

Alex laughed. "Don't rush us! We want to see what all the others think first. It's no good starting unless we have enough people to make it fun."

"We want to see how many will promise to

come," put in Penny. "Will you stay around after church and see if we can catch the Wilmot boys, and see Susan on the way back?"

Three of their friends were at the special, half-hour 'children's church' which took the place of Sunday school once a month, and was over before the grown-ups arrived for morning service.

Paul pointed them out to Angus as they slipped into their places but there was no time to talk because the hymn was just beginning.

On Sunday school mornings the children stayed for the service with their parents, but today Alex just waved to her father and mother as they drove up the lane. She ran to join Penny and Angus who were clambering over the stile.

Paul was already streaking across the field, trying to catch up with the Wilmot boys who seemed to be in a hurry to get home.

Bob was running with him, but Betty only walked and called; running was much too energetic for her.

The Wilmot boys, Donald and Fergus, were a bit doubtful when they were stopped at last and the idea was breathlessly explained to them. At eleven and twelve, they were not interested in anything they thought might be 'kid's stuff'.

"Wait till you've got everyone else rounded up, and then we'll come and see," was all Fergus would promise.

When the cousins left them they felt a little downhearted and wondered if their scheme would be a success after all, but Bob and Betty were so keen that they offered to go visiting the outlying cottages and the post office with Paul and Angus before it was dinner-time.

Alex and Penny had to hurry home. On this one Sunday in the month they were responsible for getting the meal ready by the time their parents came in, and were quite proud of their efforts at cooking. All the same, they wished they were going with the others to see what Susan said.

Penny had finished laying the table and Alex was taking her rhubarb tart out of the oven before Angus and Paul burst in, looking very pleased with themselves.

Their visiting had been a great success and Susan from the post office thought it was a wonderful idea.

In fact, they had only had one flat refusal. Rita, who lived in one of the fishermen's cottages, had to be counted out. "She has as much as she can do to get through her homework," said her mother, firmly. "I won't have her wasting her time running round with a gang."

She had shut the door in their faces with a bang —so that was that! "Pity, though," said Angus, as he watched Alex making the gravy. "We could see Rita wanted to come awfully badly."

"I've been thinking," said Alex, "that if there are eleven or twelve of us we'll have to meet somewhere. Daddy might let us meet in the big barn, but it's so cold and draughty this time of year."

"There's our bedroom," suggested Paul, hopefully.

"What! A dozen of us tramping up and down the stairs? Wait and see what Mother would say to that!"

Mother, when she was told of the idea as they

B

ate their meal, was quite in favour of the club and so was their father, but the big barn, he said, was out of the question, and the bedroom also.

"You couldn't keep the boys from playing around on the tractors," he told them, "and there's hay at the far end—I wouldn't risk somebody having matches."

Mrs Caldwell looked thoughful. In such a small place as Catlins Cove, children had to make all their own amusements when the bus had brought them home from school. She realized that the club, if it were a success, would be a wonderful interest for all of them. But, as Alex had guessed, she knew what twelve pairs of muddy feet could do.

"Suppose you meet once a week," she said, as she gave Angus a second helping of pie, "that is, during the cold weather. You could have the kitchen to yourselves on Saturday afternoons if you took turns to clean up the floor afterwards——"

"Oh, Mother, could we!" cried Alex, and Penny jumped up to give her a hug, saying, "You always are an angel about anything special!"

"All the summer you could meet in the orchard, unless it was wet," said their father, "but don't let those Wilmot boys get scrambling about my trees."

Angus finished his pie with a sigh of content. If he couldn't have his own mother and father at home with him, he thought, living with Aunt Anthea and Uncle Roger was going to be the next best thing.

CHAPTER TWO

MR BRODDIE'S BOATHOUSE

Long after Paul was sound asleep that night Angus lay awake. It had been such a busy day and there was so much to remember.

He wondered if they would ever do any of the exciting things he had read about in the book that was left in the train.

Switching on the small light on his bedside table, he reached down to the shelf underneath where he had put it, with some old annuals, in case he woke up too early.

He guessed that reading in bed at night was probably not allowed, but Aunt Anthea hadn't said he wasn't to, so perhaps just five minutes wouldn't matter.

He turned over on his stomach and propped the book on his pillow, and then for the first time saw something written inside the cover: 'This is Badger's book. Please give it back when it is borrowed.'

"Badger—that's a queer name," thought Angus. "Nickname, I expect. Poor old Badger, he won't get it back this time."

He flicked over the pages, looking at the pictures, and then he made another discovery. Near to the end of the book an envelope was hidden. Probably it had been used as a bookmark, but there was an address on it which interested Angus: 'B. A. Dodswell, Applegarth, Orchard Way, Wandford.'

Turning it over, he saw a list of names scribbled on the back: 'George Webb, Max Sellers, Archie Betts, Nobby Clark, Badger Dodswell.'

Angus was really excited now. The boy in the train had looked jolly. Perhaps he knew a lot more about camping and swimming than they did, and here was an address which must be his.

In any case, now that he had found the envelope, they could post the book back because it was evidently precious.

He heard his uncle's footsteps on the stairs and decided it was time to go to sleep. Pushing the book under his pillow, he switched out the light, and snuggled down as Uncle Roger passed the door.

Tomorrow he would have a surprise for Alex and Penny.

But of course the next day was Monday, and that meant school for his cousins, though he would not be going till after Easter.

Angus told them of his find while they had breakfast, and at once Alex had one of her brilliant ideas.

"Let's write and ask this Badger to come over one Saturday," she said. "If he lives at Wandford he could get the bus that comes by here at three and go back on the six o'clock from Dibbsend crossroads if he didn't mind walking down there."

"Why would you want him?" asked Penny, cautiously.

"Because he probably knows much more about running a really good club than we do," her sister told her, reaching for the last piece of toast. "We'd better hurry," she added, "or we'll miss the school bus ourselves."

"What are you doing this morning, Angus?" asked his aunt. "I hope you won't be lonely all by yourself."

"He needn't be," said Penny, quickly. "He could write some little notices about meeting here on Saturday afternoon and push them in the letter-boxes of all the children who said they'll join us."

"But they'll all be on the school bus, surely," objected her mother.

"If you'd ever heard the racket on that school bus, Mum, you'd know we couldn't tell them anything!" cried Alex, as she got up to search for her satchel.

"Half of us get off at the primary school and the others go on," said Penny, "which makes it difficult."

"I'll do it, anyway," Angus told them. "It'll look more official."

"Take Bess with you," suggested his aunt. "Good exercise for you both!"

Paul wriggled out of his chair and said grace for everybody. "You can use my coloured pencils, and they do better if you lick them," he added generously before he joined the general scramble for coats and berets in the hall.

Angus helped Aunt Anthea to clear the table and then she told him to get busy and write his notices.

She helped him to think out the first one and make it as short as possible, and gave him a writing pad to use.

"Make them neat," she warned him. "The parents will judge the idea a good deal by what you leave with them today. If your writing is untidy they may think the club will be rough and tumble too."

So Angus took his time, and, though he preferred to use his own pen, he ruled a neat border round each note with one of Paul's coloured pencils.

"Very nice!" said Aunt Anthea, warmly, when he showed her the result, and ten minutes later he was out in the sunshine with Bess trotting at his heels.

It was a wonderful spring morning, and the tang of the sea air added to the sweetness of the wet earth.

Angus sat astride a stile for several minutes listening to the larks singing, so high up that they were out of his sight.

Then Bess squeezed her portly form under the bottom bar, and he thought it was time he hurried on to drop in a notice for Betty and Bob.

He took a lot longer crossing the fields than they had done on Sunday because there were lambs to watch and a foxes' earth in a bank to look at, and because Bess kept straying off in different directions and he had to get her back.

He looked at his watch and saw it was nearly eleven, and he still had the cove cottages to do.

"There ought to be a short cut instead of going all the way back and round by the road," he thought. Then, in the distance, he saw a gate or a stile close to a thatched roof.

"That must be the pretty cottage Penny showed me," he decided, "and it was more than halfway to the shore."

Without any more hesitation he called Bess and

set off to skirt round by the nearest hedge in the direction of the far-off gate.

There were bullocks in that field. Luckily they took no notice of the dog or she of them, but Angus began to wonder if he was trespassing as he had left the well-worn field path.

To his relief, as he got nearer he saw that the gate had a small stile beside it, and he whistled Bess, who was lagging, and felt pleased at having found it for himself.

As he climbed over he saw a car in the lane below him. It was parked just by the twisty steps that led up to the cottage gate, and Angus could hear grunts and mutterings coming from the direction of the boot.

As he stepped into the road a man's tanned and wrinkled face appeared from behind the back wheel, and a pair of very blue eyes met his.

"It's a plaguey business, being so short of breath!" exclaimed the old gentleman, as though he had known Angus all his life, and he looked despondently at the crate he was trying to lift.

"I'll help you," said Angus at once. "If you take one side and I grab the other, we'll manage it."

He was a little too optimistic for they didn't manage it first try, but at last, with a tremendous heave, it was up.

"Well, that's your good turn for the day!" said the old man, gratefully, and then added, "That's Bess from Cove Farm, isn't it? Are you visiting there?"

"I'm going to live here for a year, anyway, with Uncle Roger," Angus told him. "And Alex, Penny and I want to start a club for the children of the cove—and Paul too, of course," he added hastily. "I'm just going round with some notices now."

"And a very good idea too. Wish more youngsters would do something sensible."

The lid of the boot was pulled down, and, showing the way up the steps, his new friend said kindly, "Come in and meet Mother. Our name is Broddie, and your Uncle Roger is a great friend of ours."

Angus was quite excited at being asked into the quaint old cottage, and Mrs Broddie came out to meet them, dusting flour off her hands.

"Come away in and sit ye down," she said in a warm Scots voice.

So Angus found himself sitting by the kitchen table, eating a scone just out of the oven.

In a few minutes he was chatting away and telling them about home and John's rugger accident, and his journey, and the book on the carriage seat.

Mrs Broddie listened and was interested, though her husband had disappeared again in the direction of the garden.

As Angus started on his second scone he began to talk about the club, well aware that he must soon go and deliver the rest of the notices.

"Well, well, ye have a grand idea," said Mrs Broddie, beginning to roll pastry. "It will be a great thing for Alex and Penny and Paul to have you with them. And where will you be meeting when you all get together?"

"Auntie says we can have the farm kitchen at present," Angus told her, "but of course when it's warm enough we can be in the orchard."

"Hum," said Mrs Broddie, thoughtfully, "you could, as long as we don't get a wet summer like the last one. I believe we might do better than that for you. Hector! Hector! Where are you? I want you a minute!"

"Coming!" called Mr Broddie, and a moment later he leaned in at the kitchen window.

"Dad," said his wife, "I have an idea for the meeting place these lads and lassies need. What about our old boathouse? It's never used now that we have the bigger one."

Angus looked at him hopefully, and Mr Broddie leaned on the window-sill and considered.

"I don't see any reason why not," he said at length, "providing they're very careful if they have any paraffin stoves and such like later on."

Angus jumped to his feet, hardly able to believe the good news.

"Would you let us have it really?" he cried. "It would be absolutely wizard! We could keep ropes and buckets and spades and maps—and—and bathing things and all sorts there!"

"Well, you'd better come and see it first," said Mr Broddie; "no time like the present! Bess seems anxious to get out of my garden, anyway, but we must be quick. I have to drive to Wandford with that box of produce."

"Oh, poor Bess!" exclaimed Angus. "I guess she's worrying about her puppies—we've been out a long time. Could I take her back, and come with Alex and Penny after tea? It wouldn't really be fair to have all the fun by myself."

That afternoon the cousins found Angus waiting for them at the bus stop by Folly Farm.

"Anything wrong?" called Alex as she jumped off the school bus.

"Wrong? No! Everything's as right as it could possibly be! We've got a club hut of our very own!"

Mrs Caldwell said she had never seen children eat their tea so quickly as the four did that night after Angus told them about his meeting with Mr Broddie.

"We've only a little while," said Alex, "because I've got masses of homework, but we simply must run down and ask Mr Broddie if we can have a quick look."

Five minutes later they were off to the thatched cottage.

Mr Broddie rose from his armchair by the fire when he saw them coming breathlessly up his steps. He took a heavy old key from a nail behind the door, and went out to meet them.

"Come along!" he said, cutting short Alex's thanks; "you haven't seen it yet. There'll be a good few spiders and earwigs for you to shift, I'm thinking!"

The cove was tranquil in the evening light as they reached the old boathouses, and two herring gulls rose from the roof of the last one as Alex turned the key stiffly in the lock and dragged open the sagging door.

Inside it was empty, except for three old barrels, a quantity of rotting rope and a long bench which ran down one side.

"That bench is really a row of lockers which you can use," said Mr Broddie, as the children looked round with delight. "Happen you'll find some odd things left inside them, but the old place should suit you fine."

"You're the darlingest man in the world!" cried Penny, speaking for all of them.

They lingered a minute or two after the old man had gone stamping away over the shingle, and already their new domain had a magical quality in their eyes.

Paul jumped on and off the bench, whooping like a Red Indian brave till Angus stopped him.

"If those are lockers, and the lids are a bit rotten, you might go right through," he warned. "Besides, now we've got this wizard place we want to take care of it."

"We must make some curtains for these funny little windows," said Alex. "And get some safe kind of lamp to hang from the rafters," suggested Penny, while Angus wondered what it would be like there when the sea was roaring on a winter afternoon.

At last they tore themselves away. "A plague on all homework," said Alex, dismally, as Paul begged to be allowed to lock the door, and swinging the key on its length of string they went home with their heads full of plans.

By Saturday the cousins could hardly wait for the first meeting of the club. Would the people who had promised to come really turn up? And would the boy called Badger ever answer the careful letter Angus had written him when he posted the book to the address on the old envelope?

Nobody but themselves knew about the boathouse as yet. It was a wonderful surprise that they were keeping to announce to the assembled company.

Alex had brought a notebook to put down the names of members, and her mother had supplied a big jug of lemonade and some biscuits for refreshments.

"We'll have to have some rules, I suppose," said Angus; "just a few so that it seems like a proper club."

"And make a list today of things we hope to do," Penny suggested, "we'd better get everyone to think of an idea and write them all down and sort out the best."

Alex reached down some glasses from the top shelf of the kitchen cupboard. "We'll be busy enough for a week or two, getting the old hut cleaned up," she said wisely, "and I guess ideas will crop up while we're doing it. I've been wondering if we could sometimes have a jumble sale for charity ..."

"Here's somebody coming!" cried Paul, who was kneeling on the widowseat. "It's Donald and Fergus, and there's Susan right behind them!"

Penny went to open the front door, and Alex sat down and set the notebook in front of her and looked businesslike.

"There's Bob and Betty coming across the field!" called Paul from his vantage point, "and they've got somebody with them—I think it's a girl."

"We're going to have too many girls," said Angus, under his breath, as Donald and Fergus came in from the hall looking terribly tidy, and surprisingly rather shy.

Bob and Betty were not in the least shy when they arrived. "This is our cousin," Betty announced. "She lives in Wandford but she comes over most Saturdays. Can she join?"

"Of course she can," answered Alex, quickly, and Susan, who was already nursing one of the puppies, said cheerfully, "The more the merrier!"

"What are we going to do?" asked Donald, eyeing the notebook suspiciously, and Fergus said doubtfully, "We shan't be able to play games much, shall we, with that big table in the middle?"

"We shan't have to bother about the table!" cried Angus, with triumph. "We've got a clubhouse all ready made!"

CHAPTER THREE

THE SANDPIPERS CLUB

There was such a hubbub of excitement and questions after Angus made his triumphant announcement that Alex had to seize a spoon and bang the table for order.

When she could make herself heard she told them of Mr Broddie's kindness, and immediately Fergus said, "Well, why don't we get down there? What are we staying here for?"

"Because two people haven't come yet," Penny told him. "They may not turn up, of course, but we'd better have some lemonade and biscuits and wait and see."

The lemonade drinking gave Alex time to write down names and ages and to add Carol Carr, the twins' cousin, to the list.

"What shall we call ourselves?" Bob wanted to know. "Every proper club has a name."

That started an argument, and ideas ranged from the Dare Devils to the Sea Wolves, but at last Susan said crisply, "I think they all sound silly—like advertisements on the telly. Why don't we call ourselves after something we see around the cove— those little birds that peck round when the tide goes out, for instance——"

"Sandpipers!" cried Donald. "Jolly good name —we'll certainly be sandy half the time and pipers make a jolly good noise, especially Scottish ones!"

So Sandpipers it was, and Alex wrote it with a flourish on the cover of the book.

"Here's Jimmie Dixon coming!" called Paul, who was still on the lookout, and Angus thought "Goodo! That's another boy!"

Jimmie Dixon should have had his brother with him, but when he joined the crowd in the kitchen it was to say that Ian didn't want to come.

"He's stuck to that old telly," said Jimmy, gloomily, as he dipped into the biscuit tin. "But there's enough here to make a jolly good club."

"Pity we're odd numbers." Angus counted them to make sure.

"Pity about Rita," said Betty. "You could see she wanted to come awfully badly. If her mother had let her, we'd have been even numbers for when we wanted to have team games."

Angus suddenly remembered something. "Didn't you talk about a girl called Vivian?" he asked Alex. "You called her another name as well."

He was surprised at the sudden burst of laughter all round the room.

"Versatile Vivian!" said Susan, with a chuckle. "We call her that at school. Whatever she hears of someone else doing she always says she can do it better! I'm sorry for her really; I think she's pretty lonely. She lives with her grandparents just beyond Folly Farm."

Alex thought for a minute and then she said doubtfully, "Well, I suppose we could try her, but I have a feeling Vivian isn't the club kind. Anyway, she's on the 'phone—would you ring Fernlea Manor and ask, Penny?"

Her sister nodded. "Good idea, and if she's interested she might cycle over right now."

Penny seemed to be an age on the telephone but at last she came back with her eyes very bright.

"Vivian actually said, 'Yes'!" she cried. "I spoke to her grandmother too. She's all for it—said it would do Vivian good. Their bailiff was there with his car, so he'll drive her over right away, and I'm sure Daddy would take her back this time."

"Wonders will never cease," muttered Susan, and although the boys were restive to get to the cove they settled down to think about what they might store in those wonderful lockers.

A sudden yelping brought them all to their feet.

"It's one of the puppies!" exclaimed Penny, dashing to the door. Bess shot through as she opened it, like a fat streak of lightning.

The cause of all the noise was one black puppy who had got himself shut out.

He was soon soothed and carried in to be petted by everyone in turn.

"I've got an idea," said Penny, as she set him down in Susan's lap. "We'll want some money, I guess, for paint and nails and curtains and things to make the hut look jolly. Daddy says we can't keep more than one of Bess's pups, but because she belongs to Alex and me we can sell the others . . ."

"And get stuff for the hut with the money?" cried Angus. "I could paint windowsills and things —Dad says I'm quite good!"

Fergus, it appeared, was a carpenter, and Carol said her mother let her use the sewing machine.

"We could have a jumble sale and make lots of money," said Betty from the hearthrug where she was cuddling Bess.

Susan looked thoughtful, and then said just what Alex had been planning to say herself.

"If we do make some money that way, or with a concert," she suggested, "I think we ought to make it for other people. Once we've got the hut just tidy, we ought to be able to be a helping kind of club."

Donald, who was sitting on the edge of the table, suddenly looked up.

"The car from the Manor is here," he said. "I saw it pass the window."

A minute later, a short stocky girl in school uniform crossed the garden towards the front door.

"Now for fireworks!" murmured Susan, as Alex went to let her in.

Alex looked with interest at the newcomer. She did not seem at all unusual, but her dark eyes had a defiant look.

"Here's Vivian," said Alex to a suddenly silent crowd of Sandpipers, and Angus was the first one to find his voice and say, "Hullo!"

"Well, tell me all about it." Vivian sat down in the chair Alex had vacated and looked as though she was ready to run the club all by herself.

But the awkward moment passed because of an unexpected arrival.

Mrs Caldwell came to the kitchen door and looked in.

"I don't think you heard the knocker just then," she said. "Here is somebody to see you who has come on the Wandford bus."

She stood back, and a tall boy with a freckled face and very curly hair stepped into the room.

Angus jumped to his feet, saying excitedly, "Why —it's you!"

C

"Yes, it's me!" answered the boy, with a sudden impish grin. "It's me—Badger Dodswell!"

At once the Sandpipers surrounded him.

"It was your book that started us!" cried Penny, and Alex and Paul said, both at the same time, "You must come and see our hut!"

"It's a boathouse!" corrected Susan, "and it's been given to us—it's all ours!"

Badger looked slightly bewildered, and Angus saw Vivian staring at him with a rather hostile look in those big grey eyes.

"Let's go down to the cove now," suggested Fergus. "There's no one else to come and there's no sense in sticking around here—we all want to see the place anyway."

There was an immediate scramble for the back door, but Alex quickly stemmed the rush.

"We've got to tidy up here first!" she declared. "It's not fair to leave Mother all those dirty glasses."

"I haven't had one," said Vivian, her chin in the air.

"So sorry!" Penny quickly poured out the last of the lemonade and handed a glass each to Vivian and Badger.

"I only like orangeade," said Vivian, and she set the glass back on the table, and gave it a push.

"And that we haven't got!" came Alex's retort quickly from the scullery beyond. "Better luck next time—you drink it up, if you want it, Paul."

She ran the tap vigorously, and Angus went to wipe up while Penny put away the biscuits.

She looked across at Angus with a glance which clearly said, "I wish we hadn't thought of asking Vivian after all."

Two minutes later they were all running down the lane and as they passed below the thatched cottage Alex waved up to Mrs Broddie who was standing in her window.

"We simply must make a success of this," she thought. "It's all happened so quickly, and we could easily quarrel and spoil it."

But even Vivian looked excited when Angus unlocked the boathouse and dragged open the heavy old door.

"This is super!" exclaimed Badger. "I just wish I lived over here—you'll have a smashing time with your club!"

"Can't you come over on Saturdays?" cried Penny. "We'll need some of your ideas before we've gone very far."

"The first idea is to clean this place up!" said Susan, before he could answer. "Look at the cobwebs and the dust—and there's a whacking big black beetle just near Betty!"

With a squeal, Betty leaped up onto the locker behind her.

"I'll squash it!" said her brother, promptly, but Badger pushed him aside.

"Hang on! It's a jolly good specimen!" he cried, and pulling a match box out of his pocket he deftly scooped the creature in.

"It seems a bit sleepy with the cold—mostly they run," he said, peering at it.

"Well, fancy wanting that!" exclaimed Vivian, her nose wrinkling with disgust. "Are you a naturalist? Is that why they call you Badger?"

"Right first time—Bernard Arthur Dodswell at your service!" he answered with a grin, and Angus cried, "Well, then, you've simply *got* to join us, because we'll need you on expeditions!"

"Well—in the holidays perhaps," agreed Badger, but they could see he was pleased.

There was not much they could do towards tidying the boathouse that afternoon. Fergus dragged all sorts of rubbish out of the lockers and made a pile of it, and they rolled the barrels to the end of the hut, wondering what use could be made of them.

"I know!" said Bob, suddenly. "If we got two planks and nailed them across the top of these old tubs, we'd have a table!"

"Smashing idea!" agreed the other boys, and Alex sat down on the locker and pulled out her notebook.

"Let's make a list of all the things we'll want, and guess what they'll cost," she said. "I can see us getting some holiday jobs to pay for everything, before we start giving to charity."

"Who said we were giving to charity?" demanded Vivian. "I thought this was a club for us to enjoy ourselves?"

"It is!" cried Penny; "but we want to do something worthwhile with it as well—even if we could only send a sizeable postal order to the 'Week's Good Cause' on the radio sometimes."

"In that case——" called Badger, who was helping Angus to get two of the barrels up on their ends, "in that case, I'll join as an associate member right now!"

Alex looked across at the two boys and felt a glow of satisfaction. She was sure Angus felt the same way as she did about the Sandpipers Club, and in Badger, it seemed, they had an ally.

She went back to her list-making, and everyone gathered round to help with ideas.

"A good stiff broom to begin with," said Susan. "It's no good borrowing one from home because we'll need it all the time."

"And a dustpan and brush," added Betty. "And nails," said her brother.

Paint, curtains, planks and a hammer were added to the list.

"And sandpaper to rub down these windowsills," suggested Angus, feeling very professional because he had helped his father.

They could only guess at the cost of most things, and were busy adding up when Jimmie Dixon, who had grown restless and wandered to the door, gave a shout.

"A seal!" he cried. "Or is it a porpoise?—it's quite close in!"

The Sandpipers poured out like a tide onto the shingle.

In the swelling water below the rocks moved a small grey head, with eyes remarkably like Bess's.

"It's a seal!" cried Badger. "A baby grey, I'd guess—I've never seen one off this coast—don't frighten him, you goof!"

He grabbed Donald's arm just as the younger boy was about to throw a pebble, and Angus said angrily, "We don't want anyone around here who chucks stones at animals!"

"I only wanted it to get a move on," muttered Donald, and Carol, who had climbed on the break-water, said quickly, "Let's make a nature diary and keep it in the locker—a seal on our first day would look jolly good!"

They watched the creature turn and glide silently out of the cove.

"Now we can skim pebbles," said Alex, not wanting to add to Donald's discomfiture, and for ten minutes they sat down in the sunshine, eating sweets which Susan had brought, and plopping stones into the calm water.

"I hope it hurries up and gets warm so that we can bathe," said Penny, and Badger looked down from his perch on the breakwater and asked, "Can all of you swim?"

"I can," answered Penny. "And I can too," said Alex. Donald and Fergus admitted to a few strokes, but Bob and Betty shook their heads.

"Daddy promised to teach me this summer," said Carol, and Angus asked, "Could you give swimming lessons, Badger? I can only do breast stroke and float."

"I'd like to," agreed Badger, quickly. "One of you at a time though, or I'd get muddled; it's a case of too many——"

He never finished the sentence, because Vivian broke in suddenly to announce, "I shan't need teaching. I've been in plenty of ships' swimming baths. Ocean liners, you know."

"Have you?" said Angus, admiringly. "Where were you sailing to?"

Badger noticed some smothered giggles among the Sandpipers, and a very quizzical look on Alex's face as Vivian answered airily, "Oh, just Durban, and Montreal, and Montreux . . ."

"But you couldn't get to Montreux by liner—"

began Susan, when she was cut short by Badger looking at his watch.

"Snakes and ladders! I'm going to miss that bus!" he cried, and in the general rush up the shingle Vivian's liners were forgotten.

CHAPTER FOUR

THE PAINTERS AND THE CARPENTERS

That week, and for several weeks to follow, the boathouse was a magnet for all of them as soon as school was over and any homework fairly done.

The days were getting longer and sometimes they played around the cove till nearly bedtime, thinking up all kinds of games when they had had enough of scrubbing and cleaning.

Susan, however, hardly ever appeared till late.

"You're not getting tired of it, are you?" asked Alex, anxiously, one day when she arrived just as they were thinking of going home.

"Tired of it?" echoed Susan. "Not likely! It's the best fun I ever had! It's earning some pocket money to help pay for our curtains that's keeping me busy. I've got myself a job at Folly Farm."

"What sort of job?" everyone wanted to know.

"A funny one!" chuckled Susan. "But it's good while it lasts! I'm feeding the sock lambs for Mrs Dodds each afternoon after school. She has ten of them, and they take her an age to feed on the bottle several times a day. She's jolly glad to be let off one feed and she's giving me tuppence a lamb every day."

"Whatever are sock lambs?" Angus wanted to know, and when he was told, "The little ones which have lost their mothers—they just mill round the orchard and bleat like anything at feeding time," he was more than envious.

"Do let me come and help you one afterooon," he begged. "I've never seen a lamb fed on a bottle!"

The others had been doing odd jobs or saving their pocket money, and at last Alex was entrusted with all the cash. She arranged to stay in Wandford after school and do their shopping, coming home on the bus which ran half an hour later.

She had to hurry to buy all the things on their list, but that night, when they spread them out on the table the boys had made, they felt she had done well.

"Saturday tomorrow," said Fergus. "Badger will probably be over, and he said he was bringing a surprise. Let's try and get the place looking nearly finished before he comes, and then we might have time for a paper chase over the cliffs before his wretched bus comes."

"Well, if we work all the morning," said Alex, doubtfully, "but painting takes longer than you think."

She had brought a dozen coat hooks, and the screws to put them up, and Angus started on the job right away.

They had added a screwdriver to their list, because, as Donald said, "They're useful for levering off lids and jabbing things, as well as for screws."

When the row of hooks was up behind the door it was rather uneven, but nobody bothered about that.

Alex and Penny held the gay blue and white material she had bought up against the windows, and Susan sheared it off with the big scissors she had borrowed from her mother.

"If we each stitch one of these and sew the curtain rings on," said Alex, "we'll have them up tomorrow. Who's offering?"

She laid aside two pieces for herself and Penny and looked at the other girls. "I'll do two on the machine," offered Susan, and Betty said she guessed she could do one if her mother helped her.

Vivian said nothing and made no move.

"That's three left," said Alex, quietly, and Bob blurted out, "If our Betty can do one, Vivian can do one too."

"I could," said Vivian, coolly, "but I don't choose to. I'm busy tonight."

She turned and hurried out of the boathouse and they heard her crunching away over the shingle.

"Well, of all the cheek!" cried Bob, and Donald said angrily, "Reckon we'll tell her she can keep away from our club if she doesn't want to help."

"Who does she think she is?" began Jimmie Dixon, but Alex cut him short.

"She's someone who just isn't used to sharing, I think," she said, "and if we send her away, perhaps she'll never learn. We'll take the extras ourselves and get up early tomorrow morning."

But as she said it, Fergus swept up the three bright lengths.

"Our mum will machine those in no time," he said; "she offered to do anything we needed, when we joined the club."

So, as they locked up the boathouse that evening, by common consent they stopped talking about Vivian.

"I'm glad we were able to get all the things before Bess's pups are ready to be sold," said Penny, with satisfaction, as she and Alex turned in at the farm gate.

"It means that almost everyone has had a hand in making the place look good, so they'll probably be more anxious to keep it tidy."

Angus had gone on ahead with Donald and his brother, but now he came panting back and joined the girls.

"I'm starving again!" he declared. "It seems ages since teatime!"

The strong sea air of the cove seemed to make Angus hungry all the time, and while she made the fishcakes for supper Mrs Caldwell thought how brown he was getting, and was glad that he seemed so content.

"This club of yours seems to be a splendid success," she said, as Alex and Penny began to turn up the hems of their curtains. "I'm sure it has helped Angus to settle here—there's nothing like having plenty to do."

Alex looked up. "It's Vivian that worries me," she said, and told her mother how near they could all get to quarrelling over her.

"Do you think we should tell her not to come any more, like Donald said?" she asked.

Angus, who had drifted into the kitchen, attracted by the smell of fishcakes, looked anxiously at his aunt to see what a grown-up would make of their problem.

"I think you were right, Alex," she answered without hesitation. "Vivian needs people of her own age terribly badly. Her grandparents are strict in one way, but spoil her in others. If you want to be a 'helping club', you have a challenge in Vivian."

"You mean it's a 'job for God', as Paul calls it?"
asked Penny.

"Well, you could put it that way!" her mother
answered, smiling, "but remember you will have
to ask God's help in trying to make her less selfish.
None of us are wise enough by ourselves to know
just what to say at difficult times."

"I reckon—" said Angus, making a pattern on
the table with the curtain rings, "I reckon I'm
lucky—my mother and dad are miles away like
Vivian's father is, but you aren't strict with me,
Aunt Anthie, and you don't spoil me either!"

"Go along with you!" cried his aunt, as she
carried a tray through to the dining-room. "I spoil
you all the time, and so does Uncle Roger! Who
had three helpings of syrup roll on Sunday? Answer
me that!"

That Saturday was a most exciting day. Angus
ran off as soon as breakfast was over and began to
work away with his sandpaper on the crumbling
old woodwork of the windows, and the other boys
drifted in one by one to help paint them with the
clean-looking grey paint Alex had chosen.

Even Paul was busy making a 'doorstep' outside
with big round stones he lugged up from the beach.

Susan arrived with her curtains and some bags of
chips to share out.

"It smells nice and new," she said, sniffing, "but
we shan't be able to hang these before Badger gets
here."

"We shall, you know!" Donald put his head in
at the window and waved his brush at her. "This is
only the undercoat and it's quick drying. If we

leave the windows open, the sun and wind will have them as dry as a bone by after dinner."

He was quite right. By the time Badger came running across the shingle that afternoon, the Sand-pipers were there in force to welcome him and the boathouse looked quite transformed.

Coats and anoraks hung on the hooks Angus had put up. A couple of cushions sent by Susan's mother graced the locker, and a shepherd's heavy lamp from the farm hung from the centre beam.

"Dad sent it," said Penny. "It's for the winter really, and he says we've always got to take it home to be filled."

"It looks super," Badger told them, looking round at the tools put neatly on ledges, and the cupboards made from orange boxes which Donald and Fergus had brought.

When Betty and Bob arrived they had Carol with them and carried a bunch of daffodils and a jar to put them in.

"There," said Betty, setting them in the middle of the plank table, "that makes it look like home!"

And then it was Badger's turn.

Slowly he undid the parcel he carried under his arm and drew out his surprise.

From a long piece of three-ply wood he had made a big nameboard, and with a fretsaw had cut out the words, 'Sandpipers Club', so that each letter stood almost free of the border.

"It's to go on the wall at the back," he said amid shouts of delight from the others. "It ought to have been coloured but I hadn't the time or the paint."

"We've got a little tin of red enamel and some black too!" cried Penny. "Daddy gave them to us because they're a bit used up. We left them at home till we found something to use them for."

"I'll go and get them," offered Angus, eagerly. "We could do it right away before we nail it up. It's absolutely wizard, Badger!"

To speed him on his way he borrowed Susan's bicycle, which she had tucked round behind the boathouse.

As he wheeled it over the shingle Vivian came slowly down from the lane.

"You're late!" he called. "But it looks smashing—you go and see! I'll be back in a minute."

"It'll look better with what I've brought," Vivian answered, and a minute later she marched in to give the Sandpipers their second surprise of the day.

"Here you are," she said. "I bought it with my pocket money!" And, unwrapping some pieces of wood joined by short cords, she laid them on the table.

"What is it?" asked Paul, promptly, while the others were so surprised at her sudden generosity that they were tongue-tied.

"A bookcase, of course—stupid! It hangs up, and the shelves hold lots of books."

At once the Sandpipers were warm in their praise.

"We'll have something to read when it comes on to rain," said Penny, quickly. "Let's find a good place for it and we'll bring down some old annuals and books tomorrow."

"She's not so bad, after all," whispered Carol to Betty. "I guess she got it at the second-hand shop, because it's pretty old, I'd say."

Meanwhile Angus was going up the sunny lane, standing on the pedals.

It didn't take him long to find the little tins of enamel in his uncle's tool shed, and he borrowed a small brush while he was there.

He was speeding past the fishermen's cottages on the way back when a door suddenly opened, and somebody dashed into the road.

Angus swerved violently, and came off the bicycle, hitting the roadway with a resounding smack.

"Rita!" he exclaimed, as he picked himself up. "You are a goat, rushing out like that! You might have hurt me badly!"

"I'm sorry!" cried Rita. "I didn't mean to—but Mother's fallen on the stove—do help me!"

Angus had awful visions of the house going up in flames, as he abandoned the cycle, and they both dashed indoors.

To his relief Mrs Cargill was lying by the kitchen table, apparently unharmed, but an upset saucepan told its own tale.

"She fell the other way but I pushed her off," said Rita, breathlessly. "Oh! do you think she'll die? She's been a bit giddy lately."

She was in such a panic that Angus had to make his voice very steady as he answered, "I think it's just a faint—looks as if she burned her arm where the stove was hot though—there's a horrible red mark coming up! Run to Mr Broddie's and tell him—he'll phone for the doctor—No—I'll go quicker, and then I'll fetch Alex; she'll know what to do!"

He turned to the door but at that moment a voice

said, "Whatever are you doing?" and Susan stood in the doorway. "What have you done to my bike?" she demanded, and then she saw Mrs Cargill and understood.

As Angus disappeared up the road even faster than he had come down it, Susan tried desperately to remember what she had heard about first aid.

"I think we'd better slip a cushion under her head," she said, as Rita stood trembling, "and undo the zip of her skirt—it looks a bit tight."

"Her arm looks awful!" quavered Rita. Susan suddenly remembered hearing her mother say one day, "If it's a burn keep the air away from it."

"With something clean," she thought, and then saw a pile of newly ironed pillowcases on the table. "Help me wrap it in one of these," she urged the younger girl, "and then put on the kettle—I believe she's coming round, and she'll want a cup of tea."

When Angus came panting back, to say that Mrs Broddie was coming down, he found Mrs Cargill sitting in a chair, drinking tea, with her arm in a make-shift sling.

"I can't thank you children enough," she kept saying, but as they went out into the sunshine again Susan was very thoughtful.

"If we're going to be a helping sort of club," she said to Angus, "we've got to know how to help properly. I was only guessing. One of the first books we ought to have on Vivian's book-shelves is a book on first aid."

"It's no good just having a book," Angus answered. "It's got to be practised—I guess that's something else Badger might teach us."

It was a crowd of very satisfied Sandpipers who closed up the boathouse that evening and prepared to escort Badger to his bus. All their work had made the old place look so nice that they were planning a party for their parents, with a camp-fire on the shingle.

"Lemonade and biscuits and buns," chanted Paul.

"And bridge rolls with cheese in them," said Alex. "We've got seven shillings left, and that would help a bit."

Then, as they trooped up the lane, they had a wonderful surprise.

Rita came running to meet them and her eyes were sparkling. She handed a crumpled note to Alex. "Please read it!" she said "My dad wrote it when he got home just now!"

The note was brief and to the point. It just thanked Angus and Susan for their prompt help, and added, "We would like Rita to join your club. You seem such a sensible lot."

"Three cheers!" cried Alex. "Now you won't be the odd one out, Rita, and we'll be even numbers again!"

They were early for the bus, and sat in a cluster on the grass verge watching the first white butterflies of the spring fluttering along the hedgerow.

"Is there anything about first aid in that book you left in the train? I didn't read it right through," said Angus to Badger.

"Not in that," answered Badger, finding a long grass to tickle Paul with, "but I've got a book I learned it from myself; I'll lend it, if you like."

"And give us lessons?" cried Penny. "As well

D

as swimming?"

"Why do you know all these things?" demanded Vivian, butting into the conversation as she often did.

"Because my dad's a missionary, I guess," answered Badger, simply.

"But what's that got to do with it?" asked Fergus, looking at him wide-eyed.

Badger stretched his long arms and gave a big yawn before he answered.

"Think for yourself!" he said good-humouredly. "If a man goes to help people in far away places he doesn't only preach to them. He's got to be a bit of a doctor, and a chemist, a gardener, and a carpenter —and a vet, very often."

"But why do you have to know things?" persisted Vivian.

"Because I hope to help one day myself," Badger told her, "and I can't help if I don't learn, can I?"

They heard the bus rumbling in the distance and he got up slowly from the sun-warmed grass.

"Jesus helped people who weren't well," said Paul, to nobody in particular.

Alex smiled at her small brother, who so often said what she was thinking. "And He helped people who were sick in their hearts, and selfish and difficult," she thought, as she looked across at Vivian. "Perhaps He will show us the way to help, if we ask Him."

CHAPTER FIVE

A SURPRISING DISCOVERY

Planning the party kept them busy for a week. It was to be a surprise, and they decided that Mr and Mrs Broddie should be guests of honour.

The surprise part of it meant that the girls could not make cakes or sweets at home, but Alex had a brilliant idea and told the cookery teacher at school about it.

The result was a cookery lesson from which she was allowed to bring back a spongecake, and Penny made rock buns and oatmeal flapjacks.

Even the boys helped. Donald was quite a good cook and he made a dozen little coffee cakes.

Fergus, with brotherly candour, said they looked almost good enough to eat.

These things, and the biscuits and rolls they had bought, were smuggled down to the hut and stowed away in tins on a Friday afternoon.

Each family of children had begged their parents to stroll down to the cove that evening, 'just to see what we've done.'

As soon as their tea was finished, the Sandpipers raced down to the boathouse to set things out, and to carry in sundry stout boxes they had collected as extra seats.

"Is your grandmother coming, Vivian?" asked Betty, as she arranged the bottles of lemonade and orange squash at one end of the table.

"She'd never get down the shingle," said Vivian, quickly, and then she stood very still as Betty went on innocently, "Anyway, there will be someone from the Manor here to see what we've all done. Your housekeeper is Carol's auntie, you know, so she's promised to come instead of Carol's mum."

Vivian didn't answer, and for a few minutes was very busy stacking the cake tins.

Suddenly there was a tremendous crash which made everyone jump, and Paul and Bob came rushing in, thinking the table had collapsed.

But it was not the table. The bookcase hung all askew, with one of the cords dangling, and the books they had collected were tumbled on the floor.

"Oh, my bookcase! It's broken!" cried Vivian, and before anyone could stop her she had unhooked it from its nail and folded the shelves flat.

"I'll mend it!" said Donald. "We want it looking nice for tonight. My dad's got some cord like that at home."

"I'll get it mended properly myself, thank you," answered Vivian, sharply, and put the whole thing hastily into the locker.

Betty picked up the books and stacked them in the corner, hoping fervently that Vivian and Donald weren't going to quarrel. But the boy shrugged his shoulders and went out to help the other boys who were building a fire of driftwood on the beach.

It was a splendid party. Mothers and Fathers, Aunts and Uncles, came crowding across the shingle at seven o'clock, and were genuinely surprised and delighted at the snug clubhouse the children had created.

Even Badger was there, for Alex was certain

that her father would drive him to the main road to catch a bus to Wandford.

Mr and Mrs Broddie were the last to come and were led in triumph to their special place on the locker.

Alex began to make a speech of thanks to them, which she had prepared very carefully, but halfway through she forgot the formal words and cried, "We all just want to say a great big thank you for this lovely place and we think you're both darlings!"

"Hear, hear!" said Mr Caldwell, and everyone began to clap.

After that the cakes and the biscuits and the wedges of spongecake vanished rapidly. Then, in the warm spring evening, they all went out to sit on the shingle round that splendid fire and sing.

Rita's father had a fine voice, and soon he was leading the 'community singing', as Rita proudly called it.

The sound of their voices went ringing round the cove as the evening darkened, till at last Mrs Caldwell said, "What about finishing with a hymn?"

"One we all know," agreed everybody, and it was Badger who suggested, "Now thank we all our God."

"Now thank we all our God, with hearts, and hands, and voices ..."

"It's a perfect choice for tonight," thought Alex, with a great feeling of contentment.

At last people began to drift away, and Mr and Mrs Broddie went back to their cottage arm-in-arm.

"It's a grand thing to see the lads and lassies happy," said the old lady. "I'm glad we had the boathouse empty for them, Hector. It's going to be an interest for us all, young and old."

With the lighted lantern hanging from the beam, the Sandpipers were clearing up and making fresh plans at the same time.

"Let's have a *hare-and-hounds* one evening," suggested Susan, and Badger said quickly, "Good idea —one half of us can go ahead and lay a trail and the others be the hunters. Not paper though; it makes such a mess. We'll use the old gypsy signs, arrows and twisted grass and stones—a 'patran', they call it."

"Much more fun!" agreed Penny. "That's a date for next Saturday, I'd say—we'll want more time than just an evening—we could have a sausage feed at the end!"

At last they began to struggle up the lane, carrying baskets and bottles.

"I say, Pen," whispered Angus, as the others went ahead of them, "I don't believe that bookcase broke at all—the cord was cut quite neatly. I saw it in the locker just now. Vivian didn't take it with her when she went home with the housekeeper."

"She probably forgot it," said Penny, but she was troubled. "I can't think who would be mean enough to spoil the thing Vivian gave us, on this party night especially."

"Donald doesn't like her," said Angus doubtfully, "but I don't think he's that mean."

Penny didn't either, but before she could say so Susan came cycling by.

"Hurry up, you two!" she called. "There's a whopping storm brewing up! Just look back at that lightning!"

It was a wet week, but by Saturday the sun was out again, drying the lilac clusters, and making the ducks go hastening to the brimming pond.

At the cross-roads the post office was busy. There were a few early visitors staying at the cottages in the cove, and Mrs Fenn's shop always drew them like a magnet.

"I'll help you unpack those boxes of soup and cheeses," Susan offered, as she ran downstairs on Saturday morning and found her mother hemmed in by a pile of newly delivered goods.

"That's nothing!" laughed Mrs Fenn. "You go and look in the garage. Coutts' driver has left all the stores for Broddies' kiosk with us—couldn't make the old people hear, he said."

"Goody!" cried Susan. "Then the kiosk will be open soon. I love helping Mrs Broddie set it out!"

Angus came in at that moment, followed by Penny with a basket and a list from her mother.

"And a pound of sausages as well, please, Mrs Fenn," she said. "We're going to make a fire and fry them on the cliffs."

"Then Susan won't need any supper!" teased her mother. "I hope you find some dry firewood after last week's rain."

Angus looked worried at that, but Penny and Susan were quite unabashed.

"We've ways and means," said Penny. "Just wait and see."

On their way down to the shore that afternoon, the cousins and Susan stopped to tell Mrs Broddie that the stores had come, and to offer to help set out the kiosk that evening.

Their offer of help was gratefully received.

"You're good neighbours," said Mrs Broddie, warmly. "I'm getting too stout for bending over those boxes."

They found the rest of the Sandpipers already perched along the breakwater.

After a little jostling and argument, they sorted themselves into two teams with Alex leading one and Susan the other.

Badger could not come that day, but his loss was balanced by the fact that Fergus had gone to the dentist.

"Pity about old Badger," said Bob; "he always gingers things up."

"We'll get him to take us somewhere for a whole day in the summer holidays," Alex promised. "I asked Dad this morning and he said we could."

She pushed her team into the boathouse and closed the door after them, promising to count five hundred and not look out of any of the windows.

Two minutes later Susan, Angus, Betty, Bob and Carol were scrambling over the rocks towards the mouth of the caves.

Susan had already scribbled a note telling where to find the next clue, and she stuck it into a cleft in some rotten old piles and ran on.

"It's jolly chilly in here!" said Angus, with a shiver, as they all entered a dark, echoing cavern.

"We're not going right through the caves, are we?" asked Betty, anxiously. "My dad says we should never come in here without torches, or without letting other people know."

"We're only going a little way," Susan told her, with a chuckle. "I've got other ideas than caves this evening. If you've never been up the Dragon's

Chimney, you're coming now!'"

Betty and Bob still looked rather worried as they all followed Susan in the cool dimness, but Angus was eager and excited.

"You'll find it's fun," Susan promised them. "My sailor brother took me up last summer. It's an awful squeeze near the top. It comes out on the cliff near the Dragon Tower."

"Will the others ever find us?" wondered Carol, as they slipped and slid on the damp floor of the cave.

"I told them in the note to come up after us," said Susan, and added with a chuckle, "I hope Vivian doesn't get stuck; she's on the fat side!"

The Dragon's Chimney was a narrow, twisty shaft. It had plenty of ledges for footholds, and also plenty of green slime on its walls.

Even Betty cheered up when she saw a glimpse of sky after she had scrambled up the first few boulders.

The glimpse was soon blotted out as Susan struggled through the narrow cleft at the top.

"Hurry!" called Angus from the darkness below. "I can hear the others laughing out on the rocks!"

At last they were all up, and scattered into the stubby gorse bushes at the foot of the Tower, while Susan laid a trail of young bracken and old brown fronds.

Then they followed her, running along the cliff path and wondering how soon the others would be after them.

But suddenly Susan stopped giggling and screamed instead. Angus was close on her heels, and to his astonishment he saw her fall forward and apparently sink into the ground.

Susan didn't go down very far. She clung to the tufty grass at the edge of the hole into which she had fallen, and in a moment Angus caught her by the shoulders and began to pull.

"Something tipped under me!" gasped Susan, as Bob joined Angus. "I feel as if I'm lying on a raft and it's still moving."

Angus knelt down and took a strong grip under her armpits.

"We'll ease you out," he said, "don't struggle. What you're lying on looks like a sort of lid ... it's thatched with heath and tufts of grass ... it's a queer thing!"

The others came panting up to help pull. "I believe it is a lid; it's made out of a hurdle!" cried Bob, catching hold of the edge of it as it moved under Susan's weight. "There's a whopping great hole under it," he added, "just like a well!"

With a mighty heave they dragged Susan back onto the turf, and then all five of them pulled the lid away.

"Why ... it's a kind of room down there!" exclaimed Angus, lying down to have a better look. "I can see two stools and an apple box. I can see how to get down too! There are holes one under the other all down this side. That pole fixed to the wall must be to hold on to. I'm going down!"

Five minutes later they were all crowded into the queer little room. It proved to have a rickety camp bed in the corner, and a primus stove and a kettle in the apple box.

But the most exciting thing was the 'window', a jagged hole in one side of the rock-walled place, which gave a grand view of the beach and the sea beyond.

"I think I know what this funny place is," said Carol, pushing Betty aside to look at the sea; "it's a bird-watcher's 'hide'. Lots of people who like wild birds come here in the summer; they're called 'orni'-something."

"Ornithologists," put in Angus, leaning over her. "I can see a black headed gull on a ledge quite close to us, and I'm sure he doesn't know we're here."

Susan started climbing the 'ladder' again, but suddenly she slipped down, saying urgently, "Quiet! I can hear the others—they're going along that path beyond the gorse bushes! We'll bob up after they've gone and give them a surprise!"

So they crouched down, smothering giggles, and heard the padding feet of their companions go racing by above them.

"I'm sure we're on the wrong track," they heard Penny say; "we ought to have caught them ages ago."

Then Vivian's voice answered crossly, "They're probably frying sausages by now!"

After the sounds died away, Angus climbed out and the others followed.

They pulled the hurdle into position again, and as Betty straightened up and pushed her hair out of her eyes she said eagerly, "Don't let's tell them what we've found! Let's keep it a secret and have them guessing if we disappear one day!"

"Good idea, but we'll tell them before the end of the summer," decided Angus, and then, dropping on one knee he exclaimed, "Look what I've found!"

They crowded round him. In his palm lay two small round objects. Coins, for certain, but not like any they had seen before.

"Someone must have dropped them," said Betty, and they looked around on the sun-warmed turf to see if there were any more.

None of them found any, but Susan, hunting in a wider circle near the gorse, called excitedly, "I've found something else—a little round case, and I'm sure it isn't old!"

They forgot about coins for the moment and went to look.

"It was in the tufty grass," said Susan. "It must open somehow." Angus took it from her and pressed and twisted till suddenly the lid sprang up.

"Why, it's a compass!" he exclaimed. "What a jolly good find. It ought to help on our expeditions. You've got jolly sharp eyes, Susan."

He gave it back and she slipped it in the pocket of her jeans.

"We'd better scram," she said; "the others will be sore if we're too long, and I'm jolly hungry."

They ran on along the cliff, deciding to show their finds but to keep the mysterious hole a secret.

"One day we could have a lot of fun with it," said Bob.

When at last they heard voices, and found the others in a grassy hollow where they had sometimes had picnics, Alex was inclined to be indignant.

"You've been ages!" she said. "We couldn't find any trail and wondered wherever you'd got to!"

"We had a bit of a hang-up when I fell over something," Susan told her calmly, and took their minds off the trail that was never laid by saying,

"Look what we found!"

The boys pounced on the compass, but Alex and Penny were more interested in the coins.

"They're ages old, I'm certain," said Penny. "Let's show them to Mr Broddie; he knows a lot about old things."

"He might by chance know someone who owned a compass," suggested her sister. "Whoever it was must be jolly sore at losing it."

The boys were inclined to say, "Findings keepings", but they were all so hungry that they forgot it for the moment and set about lighting the fire.

In this Alex, Penny and Susan were experts. They had had many holiday meals cooked out of doors, and had dry driftwood hidden away in various places along those scrub-covered cliff tops.

They replenished them each summer, and so, to the rest of the Sandpipers' surprise, there was dry kindling waiting for them in an old rabbit burrow not twenty yards away.

The cliffs dipped low there, and the boys scattered down to the shore and soon came back with extra firewood—old branches and smashed boxes lying above the tide-line where the winter gales had left them.

The fire they made was small and hot. Alex lifted a square of brown turf and showed where other fires had been made before and neatly covered again.

Betty said with a sigh of content that the sound of sausages sizzling was the nicest thing she had ever heard.

"But the smoke get in my eyes," complained Vivian, "and it stings like billy-o."

"You're the wrong way of the wind," Donald told her briefly. "Even little Paul knows to stand with the wind at his back."

"Don't tease Vivian—she wasn't born in the country like all of us," said Alex, quickly, and for once Vivian shot her a grateful glance.

They sat eating hungrily while the fire burned with a blue flame, turning to a beautiful violet shade.

"That's because it's been in salt water," Alex told Angus as she turned the last of the sausages deftly and slipped one onto Vivian's enamel plate.

"Eat up!" she said kindly. "We brought more than we needed."

Bob lay back on the turf and stared at the sky.

"I hope it stays bone dry all the summer so that we can do this lots of times," he said.

"Oh, don't wish that!" cried Penny. "What would Daddy and the other farmers do? He has to cart water to the cattle, even in the winter; ours is a terribly dry farm."

"If we had more water," said Alex, "we could have twice as much stock—it's always been a worry."

"If Badger was here," said Angus, thoughtfully, "he'd say we ought to thank God for what He sends —rain or sun or snow—and be cheerful about it, because something or somebody needs it all."

CHAPTER SIX

RITA HAS A GREAT IDEA

Mr and Mrs Broddie were surprised to see the whole of the Sandpipers Club trooping up their steps.

"Is this a deputation or something?" Mr Broddie asked, as he opened the door to them.

"Only to show you something we've found," said Alex. "We're going home to get clean, and then we're all coming to help set out the kiosk."

"We've had a smashing afternoon!" said Angus from behind her, "and found two finds as well."

Mr Broddie turned the small coins over in his horny hands. "They're Roman," he told them, "but which century I can't tell you off hand. You're very lucky youngsters. There have been some Roman remains found around the cove in days gone by, but they were few and far between."

"But how did they get on the grass?" Rita wanted to know.

"Guess rabbits kicked them out," said the old man; "they do sometimes, where there's been a cliff fall years back. You should show them to your friend Mr Fortescue if he comes with his caravan this year," he told Alex; "he'd know more about them than I do."

Susan pulled the compass from her pocket. "There was this as well," she said; "it was further on along the path. The boys want to keep it, but it must belong to somebody."

Mrs Broddie had come out to join them. "I should put a notice in your post office window, dearie," she suggested. "Maybe a visitor, maybe it's just a laddie who has saved up a long time to get it. Most everyone who stays here goes to the post office, so it could quite well be claimed."

"Thank you! We knew you'd know the right thing," said Alex, but as they went on their way Bob and Donald and Jimmie were grumbling and saying they hoped nobody ever read the notice because a compass was a smashing thing to have.

"I'll put it on my bedroom mantelpiece for safe keeping," Susan told them, "and we'll wait and see."

Penny was the first down at the cove that evening, and Susan, Angus and Rita joined her a few minutes later. Their arms were full of packages which they had carried down from the cottage.

Mr Broddie had fetched the stores from the garage at the post office in his car earlier in the day, and big cartons stood on the beach, waiting to be unpacked.

The kiosk was already set up, well under the cliff, and out of the way of the highest tides.

Rita's mother was in charge of it each summer, and she arrived later to find Alex, and most of the Sandpipers, helping Penny and Susan to set out the goods.

Alex was absorbed in sorting packets of picture postcards and putting them into racks.

"Some of these of the cove are in lovely colours,"

she said to Rita, "but some of them are awfully old. Look—there are tents on the cliff top in this one, and we haven't had any campers in that spot for years."

"Couldn't our club camp there?" asked Rita eagerly, dropping the bundle of wooden spades she was untying, to look at the photograph. "We could have a lovely time in the holidays and cook our own meals!"

"That would be marvellous!" said Angus and Penny together. "But it's not much good thinking about it," said Penny. "We haven't any tents, and I don't think Mother and Daddy would let us on our own."

"My word, I should think not!" exclaimed Rita's mother, overhearing. "I shouldn't have a wink of sleep if you were out on the cliffs by yourselves at night!"

"My brother John is coming at half-term," cried Angus. "He's much older than me, and I know he's got a tent!"

Nobody answered him because Betty called from the back of the kiosk, "Three cheers! The soft drinks are coming!"

The crunch of boots on the shingle made them all run outside to see. Mr Broddie with Donald, Fergus, Bob and Paul were carrying down the crates, which certainly looked heavy.

They all went to lend a hand, and when most of the crates were stowed under the counter Mr Broddie looked round at their handiwork.

"It looks a treat!" he told them. "Mother will be more than pleased when she comes down. She told me to tell you to have a lemonade all round, and I

E

think you deserve it. I've never seen the little old kiosk look nicer."

"Bless Mrs Broddie! I'm dying of thirst," exclaimed Alex, as Fergus began levering the tops off bottles.

"If we ever did have a camp," said Susan, hunting for the straws, "let's have it near enough to get down here for ice-lollies and things. There's drinking water too from the tap by the bathing huts— we'd need that."

"What's this about a camp?" asked Mr Broddie, sitting heavily down on a crate.

The Sandpipers sat down on the shingle beside him, sucking blissfully, and throwing pebbles for Bess to run after.

"We're only dreaming at present," sighed Penny. "We couldn't possibly camp because we haven't got any tents. I believe Dad did have one up in the loft, but it must be ages old and we'd need two or three."

Once more Angus told them about John coming. "He's got a little tent for two," he cried. "We might be allowed to camp if he and Badger shared it and came with us!"

Mr Broddie scratched the tip of his nose, thoughtfully.

"Why don't you try for a second-hand tent?" he asked. "After all, you could take turns to sleep out in it, and some of you could come over to the camp from home early in the morning. I've been trying to think where I saw a tent advertised."

"That's a wizard idea!" cried Fergus, and Angus said that Uncle Roger was bound to agree if they all begged hard enough.

"I'm sure Grandmother wouldn't let me," Vivian

decided, "and anyway tents are draughty things. When I was in the South of France——"

"Oh, when you were in China!" cried Bob, rudely, but Mr Broddie nipped a quarrel in the bud.

"I've got it!" he exclaimed. "I saw that tent in a sale catalogue this morning. There's a big house being sold in Wandford near your school, and all the furniture and contents are being auctioned next Thursday!"

"Are you going to the sale?" asked Alex, eagerly. "Dad is selling Bess's pups next week, all but the smallest, and we can spend the money any way we like. Would you—would you bid for us?"

"I can't go to the sale that day. I'm sorry, but I have to go to London. Anyway, I'll bring down the caalogue for you with the next crate of bottles."

The boys rushed off to help Mr Broddie, full of wild ideas about a camp, while the girls helped Mrs Cargill with the last of the jobs and chattered just as much.

"You would let me go, Mum, if a grown-up was there?" pleaded Rita, but her mother would only say, "I'll ask your father", and, "we'll see."

At last, tired and hungry, they went trooping up the lane, and Alex carried the precious catalogue.

"Let's all go and ask Uncle Roger together," suggested Angus, so the Sandpipers turned in at the farm gate and were delighted to see Mr Caldwell just crossing the stock yard.

"Why the crowd?" he asked, as they gathered round him, and that was a signal for everybody to speak at once.

"Just a minute! Just a minute! One at a time!"

he said firmly. "Alex, you tell me what it's all about."

So Alex told him, and Angus stood wishing so hard his uncle would agree that he got quite red in the face.

Mr Caldwell looked very thoughtful, and patted Bess in an absent-minded way as she stood up against his knee, asking for attention.

"I don't see why not," he said at last, and was deafened by their shouts.

"Quiet! Quiet!" he exclaimed. "You make so much noise that a man can't think. I have a sizeable old tent in the loft. It would do for the boys, I think —three at a time, possibly. What sort of a tent is John's, Angus?"

"It's a bivvy, Uncle—but it's big enough for two, I know!" cried Angus, eagerly.

"There's no feeling quite so grand as waking up out of doors," said his uncle, "I haven't done it for years, but I wouldn't mind sharing with John over the holiday, and I think perhaps that would make a few of the mothers happier."

"Oh, Daddy, you're a darling!" Penny gave her father a big hug. "May we try and buy that tent then? Could we go to the sale ourselves?"

"We'll go indoors and think that one out," he told her, and saying goodnight to the other jubilant Sandpipers he turned towards the house.

"I shall expect to see all of you in church, spruce and clean, on Whit Sunday morning," he called after them, and they answered with one shout, "We'll be there!"

Alex walked to the gate with Susan and Rita. "That was a most wonderful idea of yours," she said, and Rita positively glowed.

They stood there a moment in the summer dusk and Susan took deep breaths of the scented air.

"It's the meadowsweet that smells so wonderful," she said, with a big sigh of contentment. "I think your dad is super, Alex! Everything's wonderful, and it's holidays in a fortnight!"

There was quite a lot of planning to do before the day of the sale. Mrs Caldwell had been persuaded that no harm could come to the children if her husband and John camped too, and it was she who suggested a way for them to buy the tent themselves.

"It looks to me," she said, scanning the catalogue, "as if these lots and the garden tools will come up for sale about lunch time. There are usually two auctioneers at a big sale like this, so that there is no break for lunch.

"If I ring your headmistress, Alex, I think she would let you and Penny go round to Hinde House for an hour, and you could bid for yourselves. You could take sandwiches and miss school dinner that day."

So the phone call was made and it was all arranged. Then Angus begged so eagerly to be allowed to go as well that another call was made on his behalf.

"Your master says it's a great idea," Aunt Anthea told him. "He says be careful you don't bid for the wrong thing and come home with an elephant!"

It seemed a terribly long time to wait until Thursday, but the three cousins had a foretaste of excitement on the Wednesday afternoon.

By going home on the country bus instead of the

school bus, they had just half an hour to run round to Hinde House and have a look at the precious tent to see that it was in good condition.

"Isn't it an enormous hall!" murmured Penny, as they went in at the open door, following people with catalogues in their hands.

"This must be the drawing-room—look at those pictures." Alex paused on the threshold, but Angus urged her on.

"We shan't find the tent in here and we haven't much time. Uncle said it would be in the kitchen or the garden."

The kitchens and cellars were like a maze, but at last they found a white-aproned sale porter who took them to see the tent.

"It's perfect; I opened it out myself yesterday," he assured them. "If you young ones come along at a quarter to one tomorrow you might be lucky."

At least three of the Sandpipers looked enviously after Alex and Penny as they slipped out of school at lunch time next day.

A few minutes later they tiptoed into Hinde House, and stood close by the auctioneer, as garden seats and lawn mowers came under the hammer.

"Keep still, or he'll think you're bidding," whispered Angus, as Alex flicked her catalogue nervously.

"Number 367, a length of garden hose. What am I bid?" asked the brisk voice again, and Penny murmured, "Ours is the one after that."

Angus held his breath while number 368, 'A quantity of flower pots', was disposed of, and then their lot came up.

In a voice that didn't seem like hers Alex said

loudly, "Ten shillings." "Fifteen," called a hefty young man looking over the shoulders of people in the passage opposite.

"Twenty," announced Alex, firmly, and was immediately outbid by the young man who had managed to push forward a little.

Angus could hardly see at all because of a stout man in front of him, and Penny was biting her screwed-up handkerchief with excitement, as they heard Alex say, "Thirty", and then, "Thirty-five."

Suddenly there was silence. To their surprise, when the auctioneer said, "Thirty-five, I'm bid. Going at thirty-five shillings", the young man shrugged his shoulders and turned away.

"Lot number 369, the young lady by the door," said the matter-of-fact voice, and Angus forgot the crowd in his excitement and cried, "We've *got* it! It's ours!"

Several people looked round and smiled at the three as Alex led them out of the room, flushed with triumph.

"I can't quite believe it!" she exclaimed. "I was certain it would take all our money and Daddy gave me an extra ten shillings in case we needed it!"

"Only that boy wanted the tent besides us, that's why," said Penny. "Now we've got to find the porter and ask about paying."

They soon found the person they wanted, and Alex counted out the money. They arranged to call for the tent after school that afternoon.

"Here's to the most marvellous camp anyone ever had!" said Fergus, gleefully, as he helped them to lift the heavy canvas a few hours later.

With Angus on one side of the load, and Donald

and Susan carrying the poles and pegs, they made their way to the bus. Once on board they told the joyous news to their schoolmates and sang all the way home.

CHAPTER SEVEN

VIVIAN'S SECRET

They could hardly wait till the weekend to tell Badger their good fortune. The tent had been safely stowed in the boathouse, and they planned to practise putting it up on the sand at low tide on Saturday afternoon.

It was big enough to sleep three girls, so if they took turns to occupy it everybody would have a chance.

Badger knew nothing about it because he went to the grammar school in Wandford, so they kept it a secret till he reached the cove.

"Why are you all so mysterious?" he wanted to know. "You keep giggling like a lot of clowns; I'm sure you've got some kind of rag on!"

"We've got a huge surprise!" cried Paul, who was bursting with the news, and Fergus and Donald shouted as one boy, "We're going to *camp*!"

Badger was both amazed and delighted. "We're really doing things like those in my old book!" he said, as he helped them to carry the tent down to the sand and to disentangle guy ropes and set out the pegs.

They had several tries at putting it up, but found that it kept sagging in the middle because the sand was too soft to hold up the poles.

"Never mind! We know how it goes," said Alex; "we'll be able to get it up all by ourselves on Friday, while you boys are busy with yours."

"I'll be able to help out," Badger told them. "I've got a little tent of my own and it takes two."

That set the seal on their happiness because it meant that Badger could stay all the time. He was sure the guardian with whom he lived would be only too pleased to have him out of the way for a while.

Carefully they packed up their treasure, and because it was a really hot afternoon, Badger decided it was time for a swimming lesson.

There was a rush to get the boys' bathing things out of the locker, and they went racing off to the rocks to change.

The girls crowded into the boathouse and undressed at speed.

Alex was in first, swimming with strong, easy strokes and waiting till the others came tumbling out to join her.

Only Vivian sat on the shingle, looking rather sulky.

"Hurry up, Viv! There's lots of room in there to change now," said Penny, pulling a red cap over her thick hair.

But Vivian didn't move. "I don't care about swimming today," she mumbled. "My swimsuit isn't down here anyway."

Penny deftly changed the subject by tickling Rita down the spine, which sent her into the water, yelling at the top of her voice.

But Betty wasn't as tactfully as Penny. She came down the breakwater, very proud of her new swimsuit on which she had embroidered 'S' for Sandpiper. As she came level with Vivian she called across, "You can't really swim at all, can you? Why do you keep on pretending?"

"Of course I can swim, if I want to!" flashed Vivian, her grey eyes blazing. "I don't care to, that's all. Being in the club doesn't mean I have to do everything you do!"

As the others went into the water she got up and tramped off towards the caves, in a huff.

Alex, who had seen the whole thing, was troubled. "I'll just have to get Vivian alone and have a talk with her," she thought. "If she flares up at the least thing she could ruin the camp, and she seems quite keen about it now. But I'll have to be awfully wise to say the right thing to her."

Then she remembered how Solomon had asked God for wisdom because he felt that he needed it terribly badly. As she watched Badger patiently teaching Jimmie Dixon how to float, she thought that she must ask God for patience too. They would all need it with Vivian.

When the holiday came at last it was the warmest, sunniest one any of them could remember.

On Friday afternoon John arrived, a tall, dark young man, very like Angus, but without the freckles. He was burdened with a rucksack and his small tent and a guitar. As soon as his Aunt Anthea had finished giving him an enormous tea, he went down with the Sandpipers to the cove.

It took quite a lot of manhandling to get all their tents and gear up to their cliff-top campsite. Luckily they did not have to go to the caves and up the Dragon's Chimney to get there, for a flight of wooden steps went up from the shingle quite close to the boathouse.

It was a wonderful spot they had chosen, almost in the shadow of the Dragon Tower.

Thick clumps of gorse sheltered them from the cliff path, and they were close enough to the steps to be able to go down to the tap for water and to the kiosk for biscuits and sweets.

It was tremendous fun collecting driftwood for the fires and getting the camp all shipshape before Mr Caldwell came to share their supper and spend the night.

Penny and Susan and Betty were the three lucky girls to share their tent the first night, and they felt quite sorry for Alex, Vivian, Rita and Carol as they went down the steps on their way home.

"It's lucky Viv doesn't want to sleep out here at all," said Angus, watching them go. "It means that it's all nice and neat—three girls each night. It's wizard that Badger has a tent for two, because none of us boys has to go home."

"Trust the boys to be in clover," Susan told him, as they wandered back to where the dying embers of the camp fire glowed between the tents.

Susan and Penny made a last cup of cocoa for everyone before they turned in, while Betty saw that all the beds were ready and comfortable.

John fetched his guitar from the little green tent which stood next to Badger's, and as they sat enjoying their hot drink he began to play. Folk songs first, ones that they knew and could sing, and then, when Mr Caldwell had said a simple prayer, they all joined in, 'Now the day is over'. Even Paul and Bob knew all the words of that, and, as he sat singing and watching the bats swooping low, Angus thought what a perfect day it had been.

Everyone went for rather a chilly swim early on Saturday morning, and then even getting breakfast and washing up afterwards was fun.

As the day went on, Alex couldn't help noticing how often Vivian contrived to be absent when there was wood to chop or rubbish to bury. She was equally adept at being present when ices were to be fetched from the kiosk.

Mr Caldwell had had to go back to a busy day on the farm, but John and Badger took on the leadership naturally, and nobody questioned their authority.

It was Badger who suggested that they walked inland to Pitt's Woods where the bluebells were wonderful to see, and where there was one huge old tree which was just perfect for climbing.

"Let's take our ropes," said Angus. "We might make a swing if the branches are tough, or just have it to swarm up and see how high we can get."

"What about cooking dinner?" asked Vivian, showing unusual interest in an everyday job.

"Bully beef and bread, and bananas today, my dear!" John told her. "No frills till tonight and then we'll go mad and have tomatoes and spuds with our sausages. I worked it all out with Alex over breakfast!"

Vivian looked glum, and as they went chattering up the chalky path that would lead them over the downs she lagged behind all the way.

Soon the woods lay below them in the valley, and they could see such a long way that the farm and Mr Broddie's cottage and the sweep of the cove looked like a model landscape with toy buildings.

"Now you can see how dry Daddy's land is,"

Alex said to Angus. "Look how chalky the fields are, and what little stubby hedges divide them. He really worries about it sometimes because it's such an awkward bit of country."

"It's beautiful though," said Angus, and then he began to run after the others. "Hurry," he called, "or they'll be up that tree first!"

The great tree was all that Badger had promised and soon the Sandpipers were swarming up into the branches, followed by some cautionary shouts from John.

All except Vivian, that is. She seemed to be more interested in picking bluebells, till Susan's voice hailed her from among the leaves.

"Hey, Viv!" she called. "Bring us up that long rope, will you? We've left it on the ground by mistake. It's easy climbing the first bit, and then I'll give you a hand up to where we are!"

Vivian looked up and stood very still. Her face turned first very red and then very white. Suddenly she swung round and began to run, crashing through the undergrowth and leaving the Sandpipers silent with astonishment for a moment.

John had gone exploring further into the woods, so he was not there to see her sudden flight.

Angus was well out on a great spreading branch but he acted quickly.

"I'll go after her!" he exclaimed and, working along to where it dipped low over a ditch, he let himself drop into a heap of dry leaves.

It wasn't difficult to follow the fugitive for he could hear her crashing on, till breathless and sobbing she threw herself down in a little clearing.

Angus came panting through the hazel bushes

and sat down beside her.

"You silly little chump, Viv! What did you do that for?"

Vivian didn't answer, so Angus tried again. "Was it because you hate climbing trees? Or are you getting tired of the club? If you don't tell us, we can't help you. Alex and Penny want to help you—we all do."

Again silence, and then he heard Vivian whisper, "I'm scared of climbing . . . I'm scared of water, and I'm scared of the dark too! But most I'm scared that everyone will think me a coward, and so they won't like me. They don't like me at school either—nobody does!"

Angus was quite dumbfounded. He had never imagined that Vivian's boasting covered up such a deep sense of being unwanted.

He stared at her shaking shoulders, trying to find the right thing to say.

His mother's words to him before she went away flashed through his mind—"Always tell God when you are in a difficulty."

In that moment of silence he was saying in his heart, "Please, God, help me; she's so awfully miserable."

"Oh, do stop crying!" he said aloud. "You're an awful silly, you know, because nobody would mind if you said you couldn't do things. It's pretending that puts everyone's back up. Nobody minds if you say honestly that you're scared either. Most everybody's scared of something. I'm scared of earwigs."

Vivian sat up, her face smudged with tears.

"I've got to make them think I'm worth knowing somehow," she mumbled.

"But listen!" urged Angus. "Nobody ought to make up stories about being able to do things when it just isn't true! And being frightened of things isn't being a coward; it's trying to be brave that counts! All the club wants to like you, and they'd all help if you gave them a chance. Why don't you ask God to help you not to be afraid, Viv? He would, you know!"

Vivian stared at him, her grey eyes very wide. "Do you believe that really?" she asked in an uncertain voice.

"Of course I do!" he said stoutly, "and my favourite text is 'Be strong and of a good courage'! It goes on to say you can be brave because God is always with you. You ask Alex—she's certain too. She'll explain a lot better than I can."

"'Won't they tease me if I come back now?" asked Vivian, after a moment's silence. "I'd like to ask Alex, but are you sure she'll bother with me?"

"Absolutely a hundred per cent certain," Angus told her, and catching her hand he hauled her up.

"Come on!" he urged. "Hurry! I'm starving and I know Penny has apples and biscuits for us in her school satchel."

The Sandpipers had left the big tree by the time they got back. John had found a woodpecker's nest in a hollow stump and they had all rushed off to see it, forgetting their idea of making a swing.

Angus and Vivian could hear their voices beyond the hazel coppice and soon found them, with Badger scribbling away in the nature notebook.

No one asked Vivian why she had run off and Penny dealt her out biscuits and an apple as though nothing had happened.

It was when they all started back along the down-land path that Angus managed to get hold of Alex and see that she walked with Vivian, letting the others get ahead.

"Viv wants to explain why she ran off," he said briefly. "She's in a bit of a bother and I said I was sure you'd help her."

Very flushed and ashamed, Vivian blurted out her story. "I even pinched that bookcase from Grandma's loft," she mumbled finally. "I wanted to give something that looked grand, so I said I'd bought it. That's why I had to cut the cord and hide it when I knew our housekeeper was coming to the party!"

"Well, of all the ..." began Angus, in surprise, and then he checked himself and exclaimed, "I knew it was cut; I thought one of the others did it to tease you."

Vivian shook her head miserably, and Alex said quickly, "You'll feel a whole lot better now you've told us about it, but it's telling God you're sorry that counts. If you're really sorry and tell Him so when you say your prayers tonight, He'll under-stand and forgive you. Then you'll never want to do things like that again. You see, when Jesus died on the cross long ago, He died so that we can all be forgiven if we believe He is our Saviour."

Vivian trudged along in silence for several minutes and Angus kicked small lumps of chalk ahead of them, not knowing what to say next.

"I know that's true, because I've done bad things myself," said Alex, gently, "but since I asked Jesus to let me belong to Him for always I've been a whole lot happier, and knowing that Jesus died for

F

me makes me want to love and serve Him. Why don't you try it, Viv? Say your prayers slowly and think what you're saying, and remember to say, 'Thank you', when nice things happen to you."

"I don't generally say my prayers at all," confessed Vivian. "But I go to church on Sundays. Gran makes me," she added defensively.

"Well, keep it up!" Alex told her, cheerfully, "and start praying as well. Don't just go because your gran makes you either; go because you know you belong to God, and you want to be with all the other people who belong too!"

She smiled at Vivian, and her warm, friendly look made Vivian feel just a little bit better.

"I'll try," she said at last, "if you really think God wants me to belong."

"I'm certain sure He does," said Angus over his shoulder, and he added, "I'm going to catch the others up—come on—run!"

With a feeling of relief the two scampered after him. They could see the other Sandpipers far in the distance, and hunger spurred them on.

Only once did Angus slow down, and then it was to call back to Vivian, "I guess you'll have to put the bookcase back where it came from, so I'll see if I can make another one!"

John had a surprise for them all as they ate their rather spartan meal.

"*Hide-and-seek* for everyone this afternoon!" he said; "that is, if you like my new version of the game! I've got some prizes of sorts, and I'll hand them out to anyone that Badger and I can't find in twenty minutes! How's that?"

"Wizard!" cried Fergus. "But you'll give us a

decent start, won't you? It takes a bit of doing to find a really good hide."

They were all delighted at the idea but Angus and Bob seemed especially so. Susan, who was sitting next to Angus, gave him a meaning nudge, and Betty and Carol were giggling so that they nearly choked.

When the meal was over and the camp was made tidy, the five of them bunched together declaring that they should be counted as one team.

"All right," said John, innocently; "then Alex had better take all the rest—I hadn't thought of having teams for this, but there's no reason why not."

Putting his fingers in his mouth he gave an ear piercing whistle and the Sandpipers scattered in all directions.

Angus headed straight for the cliff path with Betty behind him, but Susan had the sense to dash off in the opposite direction and she came back to join them after Alex and Penny had disappeared behind the Dragon Tower with Fergus, Donald and Vivian at their heels.

Rita had vanished so quietly that nobody saw her go.

Angus reached the secret 'hide' first and was dragging the lid off when Bob and Susan joined him.

One by one they scrambled down and Carol came last, panting and speechless. Two minutes later, with the 'roof' pulled over their heads, they stood looking out of the rocky little window onto the beach below. There were quite a lot of visitors down on the sand, but nobody looked up.

"Someone has been here lately," said Betty; "there are some empty tins that weren't here before."

"Hush!" whispered Angus. "I can hear Badger!"

Badger was talking to John and they passed so close that Susan was afraid their sharp eyes would spot the 'lid'. But they went by, and the five breathed again.

"The twenty minutes is nearly up," said Susan, looking at her watch, "but we'd better wait another minute or two so that no one spots us coming out."

There was nobody about when they scrambled up into the sunlight again, and they trotted gleefully back to camp.

Everyone else was there except Rita. "Well, you've certainly won hands down," John told them. "We thought you'd vanished off the face of the earth!"

"So we had!" began Carol, but Angus pinched her. "Don't tell yet!" he whispered. "We can probably have some more fun and we're not upsetting the old bird-watcher!"

Alex and Penny and both the boys had been found, but much to her joy Vivian had remained hidden by crawling under the canvas which John had spread over their stores.

"Well done, you!" he said, as he handed out chocolate bars to all the lucky ones. "I've got two left, and one must be for Rita—I wonder where in the world she's got to!"

"We'd better all spread out and search—" began Badger, but suddenly Angus shouted, "There she is!"

And there she was, coming slowly from the direction of the gorse bushes, looking so small and woebegone that Alex flew to comfort her.

"I—I got stuck under a gorse bush and I couldn't get out!" she sobbed, showing her torn dress and her arms and legs covered with scratches.

"Oh! poor Rita!" There was a chorus of sympathy as they crowded round her. "The two chocolate bars for you, definitely!" said John. "And you'd better get Alex to do some first aid—I know she's got all the kit, and knows what to do with it."

Susan beckoned to Angus and Betty and for a moment they whispered together.

"What's the secret?" asked John, as he searched for the mallet to tighten some tent pegs.

"A whopping secret!" answered Angus. "The secret of where we hide, and we're going to let Rita share it just to cheer her up!"

CHAPTER EIGHT

A LIGHT IN THE TOWER

Rita had a job to keep smiling for the rest of that hot day. Her scratches were deep and painful, and when they all went swimming before supper she had to come out. The salt water stung unbearably.

Angus and Susan took her off to see the 'hide' while the others were busy with the camp fire, and she forgot her discomfort for the moment in marvelling at the little, hidden place.

"I don't like it much though," she said, with a shiver. "Suppose it isn't a bird-watcher that made it!"

"Perhaps it's someone's idea of camping," suggested Angus, but for the first time he wondered if there could be a more sinister reason for the secret place.

"Let's get back to the others," he said. "Perhaps we ought to show it to John or Uncle Roger after all."

"Oh, not yet!" cried Susan. "It doesn't matter who it belongs to. We could always stop coming here if anyone told us not to."

So they asked Rita to keep their secret, and ran back to find the supper nearly ready.

"There's Dad coming along the path," called Penny, as they joined the others. "I guess he's just had his supper, but he could probably eat an extra sausage!"

It was a wonderful starry night by the time they were all tucked up in bed. Vivian had gone away down the cliff steps with Susan, Penny and Betty directly after supper, but not before she had whispered to Alex, "Thank you for helping—I won't forget."

Alex, Carol and Rita lay looking out beyond the tent flap, and listening to the squeaky sound of a mouth organ which came from the boys' tent, till a wrathful shout from Mr Caldwell caused sudden silence.

It was wonderful, Alex thought, to feel the cool night air on her face and to hear the owls calling in the woods behind them.

Rita thought so too, but the discomfort of her arms and legs kept her from settling.

From where she lay she could see the gaunt outline of the Dragon Tower, and presently she realized that Alex was awake as well.

"Are your scratches bothering you?" whispered Alex.

"They're awful!" Rita moved restlessly. "I just can't get comfortable," and then suddenly she said, "I say—can you see what I see? There's someone on top of the Tower!"

Alex sat up. "There can't be! Even holiday-makers wouldn't be around at this time of night!"

"I saw someone move!" insisted Rita, but Alex was unconvinced. "It could be a trick of the moonlight," she suggested, and snuggled down again.

Rita lay down too, but she was still wakeful.

Suddenly she sat up again, rubbing her eyes, and staring at the Tower.

From behind the battlements came some quick

flashes of light, and then darkness again.

"Alex!" whispered Rita, urgently. "Alex! There's a light up there now!"

But there was no answer. Alex was fast asleep.

Rita lay awake a long time, and in the morning she told Badger about the mysterious light. Badger said unfeelingly that she was dreaming.

"Those scratches gave you a nightmare," he assured her; "come and give us a hand to fetch the water for breakfast."

The girls who had slept in camp were cooks for the morning. When the others arrived full of good cheer, and bringing some eggs from the farm, they promptly went off again to bathe, and the boys were already in the water.

"I wish I was too!" sighed Carol. "I just can't get this fire to burn properly, and the billy-can keeps tilting."

She expected a sympathetic answer from Alex but when she glanced up Alex wasn't in sight. Somebody else was! A tall young man with very red hair was walking down the little track between the gorse bushes.

"Do you live around here?" he asked abruptly, as he stopped between the tents.

"Down in the cove," answered Carol, shyly. "Most of us are down bathing."

"Are you camping for long?" the young man wanted to know, and Carol thought he looked far from pleased.

"Only over the holiday," she told him, and to her relief the man turned and went back the way he had come, just as Alex came back with her arms full of driftwood.

"What did that person want?" she asked.

Carol told her. "I guess he was just on holiday and being inquisitive," she said, and at that moment a loud hissing told them that the billy-can had tilted still further, and their visitor was forgotten.

All too quickly the glorious camping days slipped by. Alex and Angus were particularly pleased to notice that Vivian was trying to be helpful and seemed to be checking her boastful speeches.

Badger remarked on it to Alex. Even he had noticed how much less troublesome Vivian was.

"I'll tell you why," said Alex, and she briefly told him of Vivian's loneliness, without making any mention of the stolen bookcase.

They were sitting on the rocks, exhausted after a game which John called, grandly, *Water Hockey*. Badger looked across to where Vivian and Paul were chasing each other with long strands of seaweed.

"She looks happy enough now," he said thoughtfully, "but she'll want a bigger anchor than just the club, I guess, if she wants to stay happy."

"I've told her that she can always be happy if she knows she belongs to God," answered Alex, knowing that Badger would understand.

"She wants friends more than anything," he said quickly. "She told you so, and that should help her to take a special text and make it her own. I'll look it up for you and you can tell her. I think it's in St John's Gospel but I'm not certain."

"About friends? I know it!" Alex searched her memory for a moment and then said triumphantly, "It's one my grannie used to tell us about. Jesus said to His disciples, 'Ye are my friends', so anyone who follows Him has a friend for always!"

"Well, get that over to Vivian, if you can," urged Badger, slipping down off the rock. "Come on; there's John yelling for us. I think they're going to have a tug-of-war!"

Susan too was doing her best to make Vivian feel wanted. Angus had asked her to do her best, so one morning she made a point of asking her to help collect some bread and sausages from the post office shop.

"Of course I'll come!" said Vivian, quickly, and Susan was delighted to hear her singing 'The Road to the Isles' as they pedalled up the lane.

It was very useful to have a couple of bicycles locked in the boathouse during these camping days, and everyone but Paul and Bob took turns to ride them.

The post office shop was busy already. "You'll find your bread in the back room," said Susan's mother. "There's no need to ask if you're enjoying yourselves; you look as brown as gypsies!"

They stuffed the loaves into their beach bags, and added some crisps and popcorn.

"You might take this brown loaf down to Mrs Broddie; I promised to keep her one." Susan's mother slipped it into a bag, and then added, "By the way, someone claimed that compass you found on the cliff a while ago. Said he'd seen the notice in the window, but I made him describe the case and say what size it was before I gave it to him."

"The boys will be disappointed!" sighed Susan. "Fergus, for one, was certain it would never be claimed! What sort of person had it?"

"A young man; very red hair," said her mother, briefly. "Now get along with you; you're filling up the shop!"

"Sounds like that man Carol told us about," said Susan, as they cycled away. But Vivian couldn't hear; she was whizzing down the lane, far ahead.

She remembered to stop at the thatched cottage, and leaning their cycles against the bank they ran up to deliver the brown loaf.

But when they went into the low, cool kitchen they found that the usual peace of the little cottage had been rudely upset.

Mrs Broddie, looking very white and strained, was leaning back in the big armchair, while her husband, with some agitation, was speaking on the telephone.

"What is it? What's happened?" asked Susan, anxiously.

Mrs Broddie tried hard to smile as she answered, "I don't quite know—I slipped. I seemed to twist my back somehow, and they're whisking me away for an X-ray. Hector is ringing up about the ambulance now. I just hate leaving him," she added; "he's as helpless as a bairn, on his own."

"Don't you worry!" exclaimed Susan. "We'll all look after the cottage, and Mr Broddie as well! Some of us can cook quite well, and I know it's what our mothers would want us to do for you both. We'll feed the chickens and the cat today, if Mr Broddie is going with you."

"I'll wash up these plates and saucepans right away," said Vivian, quietly, as she noticed a pile on the draining board. To Susan's surprise she began, a little clumsily, to do the job she had always avoided.

"You're good lassies, both of you," said the old lady, a little shakily, and as Sue settled the cushions more comfortably behind her head she felt that the Sandpipers Club had their first real 'helping' job.

In the days that followed Mrs Broddie's accident the whole of the club did their best to repay the old couple's kindness to them.

It was decided that Mrs Broddie must stay in hospital for at least a fortnight, and the hospital was so far away that her husband had to spend a long time on his visits.

He was very relieved to find that the girls, between them, could keep the cottage neat and shining, while the boys saw to his livestock and watered his plants.

The camp of course had to come to an end in any case. There was school once again, and John had to go back to college, but they all decided it had been the most glorious week of their lives.

By getting up extra early to do homework, the Sandpipers were free to go to the thatched cottage directly after tea each day, when Mr Broddie was already gone to pay his evening visit to his wife.

Only Betty did not seem to be pulling her weight, Alex reflected one day, as she took a bucket and leather and began to clean the little diamond-paned windows which Mrs Broddie always kept so bright.

It was understandable though, she thought, because Betty's mother had just bought the last of Bess's pups as a birthday present for her, and Betty could not tear herself away from it. She had brought it to the cottage once, saying it could play around while she worked, but it had chased the cat and chewed the kitchen hearthrug.

"Where's Angus got to?" Alex asked Penny, who was laying the table for Mr Broddie's supper.

"He said he was going up to our camp site to look for that old silver pencil his father gave him," answered her sister. "He thinks he lost it while they were taking the tents down—he's looked everywhere else."

Angus came in at that moment, looking despondent.

"No use," he said, "and I hate losing it because Dad had it when he was a boy. But I found something else," he added; "another of those funny old coins I found before. I've got the others in a matchbox, and now I've found this one we can have one each."

"Good old Angus; you're always good at sharing," said Penny, but she added with a sigh, "I wish we could find a real hidden treasure, or have another adventure of some kind. It seems a bit dull now that camp's all over."

She little knew that the next day would be anything but dull.

It was a different kind of morning in any case because Mr Caldwell set off for London early to go to a big meeting of farmers and stockbreeders.

Mr Broddie too was away. He took the opportunity to go up to town with Mr Caldwell while his wife was safely cared for.

Everything at the farm was left in charge of Mr Coutts the cowman.

"And even Mummy is going to be away this afternoon," said Paul at breakfast. "We'll be like people on a desert island!"

"Not quite as bad as that, I hope!" laughed his mother. "It's unfortunate that the group meeting of the Women's Institute should happen today, but there it is. I'll be back in time for supper."

They all trooped off to get the school bus, knowing that there would be something for their high tea in the fridge, and that Alex was to look after them till Mother came home.

As usual other Sandpipers were waiting at the cross-roads, but, when Betty came to join them, her face was smudged with tears.

"My Sandy's lost!" she sobbed. "He ran away last night while I had him for a walk and he hasn't come home this morning!"

They were all sorry for her, and concerned for the puppy, especially Alex and Penny, because Sandy had been the smallest and most spoiled of Bess's pups, and so the last to be sold.

"Which way did he go?" asked Vivian, sensibly, and Betty hung her head.

"I—I don't know," she confessed; "I tried playing hide-and-seek with him round the boathouse, and when I came out to look for him he just wasn't there."

"But he's only little!" began Susan.

"He can run fast though," said Betty, quickly. "He followed me all along the top of the cliff on Saturday, and came down the steps as good as gold."

At that moment the school bus lumbered up, and they climbed on board promising that they would have a puppy hunt in the evening when Mr Broddie's hens were fed.

"We'll meet you at the boathouse," they told Betty, "and then we'll fan out in all directions."

"I shan't," said Vivian, quickly. "I have to stay in till later—Grandma has visitors, and I have to stay and be polite."

She made a face and said gruffly, "I hate being polite."

"So do we!" called Fergus and Donald, with sympathy, from the front seat.

The thought of the puppy nagged at Penny all day. She hated the idea of him wandering and lost. She would have started to look for him without any tea when they got home that afternoon, but Alex was insistent.

"It's stupid to go out hungry," she said; "we may be out ages. I'll leave a note for Mummy, telling her about Sandy, in case we are."

Angus needed no persuasion to eat, but halfway through tea he suddenly jumped up.

"I know where one thing is!" he cried. "I've just thought of it! My silver pencil! It's in our hide. I haven't seen it since we showed the place to Rita, and I know it was in my pocket then!"

In fact all the Sandpipers had been shown the hide on the last afternoon of camp and there had been much climbing in and out.

"Well, we'll go up there tomorrow," began Alex, but Angus wasn't waiting. "I've had enough to eat," he cried, "and if I dash up there now I'll be back by the time you've finished and washed up!"

"I'll come too!" began Paul, but Angus was gone with a slamming of doors, and Alex said, "Well, of all the chumps! As if he couldn't wait! It's lucky Fergus and Donald are feeding Mr Broddie's chickens today."

They finished their own tea and cleared the

table, but there was no sign of Angus. "Well, I'm not waiting for him," said Penny. "He knows we're looking for Sandy so he can just start looking himself when he gets back."

They started down the lane, wondering if Betty would meet them at the boathouse to tell them that the puppy had been found while they were at school.

But she was not there and neither were the other Sandpipers, so they decided to begin by looking underneath the kiosk and all the beach huts in case Sandy had got wedged there. Bess was with them and she sniffed about anxiously, as though she knew something was wrong.

But there was no sign or sound of a little dog, though they hunted in every corner and under all the upturned boats.

Suddenly Penny cried, "Here's Angus! Look how he's running!"

"What's the matter?" asked Alex. "Anything bitten you?"

Angus certainly looked bothered.

"It was the hide," he panted. "I was quite close to it when suddenly I saw the lid move and begin to lift!"

"What did you do?" asked Paul, aghast.

"I dashed behind the gorse bushes and watched," said Angus, "and a man looked all round and then climbed out—a tall man with red hair!"

CHAPTER NINE

THE MYSTERY SOLVED

Angus sat down on an upturned boat and told the rest of his story.

"After the man had walked past me," he said, "I was afraid to go to the hide in case there might be someone else down there, so I did a bit of stalking and followed him!"

"Go on!" they said eagerly, and Angus explained how he had watched the man go down the cliff steps and turn towards the caves.

"Then I had an idea," he said. "If I wriggled down the Dragon's Chimney I should see him if he came in there and perhaps find out what he was doing. I had to be quick—and quiet. I meant to climb out and run like mad if he saw me, but I had another fright because a tall boy, about John's age, came in too, and they sat down on a boulder and started talking. I was so scared, and afraid that I'd sneeze or kick a piece of rock down, that I can only remember half of what they were saying."

"People aren't supposed to listen to other people," said Paul.

"But that wasn't like listening at doors," protested Angus; "there's something queer about these men; they might be smugglers!"

At that moment crunching shingle told them that someone was coming, and Fergus and Donald appeared from behind the kiosk.

G

Betty and Bob came running from the other direction, with Susan just behind them.

"Have you found Sandy?" called Paul. "We've found some smugglers!"

"We haven't!" said Alex quickly. "We don't know a thing about them yet!"

Sandy had not been found and Betty and Bob both said that it was no good hunting any more.

"Our dad spent the whole of his lunch hour looking, and he's phoned the police at Wandford in case he was taken there by anybody," Bob told them.

"He says maybe someone saw him running and just took him away in a car," said Betty, tearfully. "He says it was all my fault for not keeping an eye on him."

"What's this about smugglers?" asked Fergus, abruptly changing the subject, and Angus had to tell his story all over again.

"But what did they say that made you think they might be up to no good?" demanded Alex. "You can't imagine people are smugglers because they come out of the hide and go into the caves—we do both those things ourselves!"

"One of them," said Angus, thinking hard and trying to remember, "one of them said, 'Well, it wasn't a success, was it? I tried to keep the boat coming steady towards the light, but there was nowhere one could land on that bit of the cliff.' The other one said something about being too high up on the Dragon Tower and that he'd waved the light to and fro."

"So Rita *did* see a light in the tower!" cried Penny. "It wasn't just a nightmare because of her scratches!"

"We've just got to find out what the light was for!" cried Fergus. "We went into the old Tower heaps of times when we were camping, and there's nothing there except a lot of rubble and those old stone stairs up one side."

"There might be something hidden there now!" exclaimed Angus. "One of them said, 'What we want is up there; we've just got to do the job before someone else does.'"

They stood round him, feeling excited and a little frightened at the same time.

"If Daddy was at home I'd go and tell him about it," said Alex, but Donald cried, "Oh, no! Don't let's spoil it by telling grown-ups—let's find out ourselves and tell them afterwards!"

"What about Mr Fortescue?" suggested Susan, disregarding him. "I saw their caravan in Morton's meadow this morning, so they've come for their usual fortnight."

"Cheers!" cried Alex and Penny both together, and Alex added, "I'm glad they've come. We'll go up and have a scout around the tower ourselves, but we may find we need a grown-up after all."

In the end it was decided that Susan should cycle back to Morton's meadow and tell Mr Fortescue about the mystery, while the others went to the cliff top to see what they could find out.

"We'll just be playing some game or other if we come across the red-haired man," said Penny. "He won't suspect that a gang of children playing on the cliff top are interested in his doings!"

They climbed the cliff steps, warm in the evening sun, and left behind the few bathers splashing in the shallows, and Rita's mother putting up the shutters at the kiosk.

There was nobody on the cliff path and the Dragon Tower stood silent and lonely on its commanding height.

"It's good having something as old as this on Daddy's land," said Penny, "but I hate to think that smugglers were using it for something bad."

"Is this all Uncle Roger's land?" exclaimed Angus, with surprise.

"Right along as far as the gap where we picnic," Alex told him, "but of course his fields only begin in the dip behind the tower—he's always left this bit wild and open for everybody to enjoy."

Fergus was far ahead of them and they saw him disappear into the ruined old doorway which faced the sea.

A moment or two later the others were crowding in as well.

At first the ancient place looked exactly as they always knew it. Just the thick rubble on the floor, and the old stone steps rising up to giddy ledges high above their heads.

Jackdaws flew in and out of gaping holes and croaked and called all the time.

Fergus was going methodically round the walls searching for any loose stone which might conceal a hiding-place for smuggled goods.

"Someone *has* been poking about here!" he said, as the others crowded in. "The rubble has been shifted back from the foot of the wall in several places—see here!"

"It looks as if the floor had been dug up and put back again just near the door!" exclaimed Alex. "We can't find out if there's anything buried though, unless we go home and get a spade."

Betty shivered. "Suppose the men came and found us digging!" she said fearfully. "I do hope Susan comes soon with Mr Fortescue."

They all felt a bit edgy, as though there was something mysterious very close to them in the Dragon Tower, and they were made even more jumpy when Angus exclaimed, "There's a voice calling—I'm certain. Listen! It's underneath us somewhere!"

They listened, and even Alex shivered a little, but none of them could hear anything except the jackdaws and the gulls that wheeled overhead.

"You're imagining things!" Betty edged towards the door, and Paul ran outside saying, "I want to go home!"

"We'd all better go home," decided Alex. "We just can't do anything here without help. We may meet Susan and Mr Fortescue on the way down and tell him the floor looks suspicious. He'll know what's best."

They were all glad to get out in the sun and ran towards the cliff steps even faster than they had come. All except Angus. He was still sure that he had heard a voice calling, and that it had not been a seagull's cry.

He let the others get ahead of him, and then he quietly slipped behind some gorse bushes and ran swiftly back.

This time he went round the outside of the tower. Thick clumps of brambles grew close to its walls and a great mound of grass-covered chalk closed it in at the back.

Keeping near to the wall Angus burrowed low

under the bushes, and to his surprise he found a regular tunnel below them and a well-worn track.

Somebody had come this way very often.

Angus hesitated. If this was a much-used path, somebody might be ahead of him in the shadows. He was just about to turn and crawl back when he heard the voice again. Faint but clear, it was calling, "Help!"

He hesitated no longer. "I'm coming! Where are you?" he called, and waited for the answer. "Down here—I've hurt my leg—but I've got Sandy!" came the voice from somewhere in the gloom ahead.

"Why, it's Vivian!" cried Angus, and he went forward with such speed that he realized only just in time that he was on the edge of a gaping hole.

"How do I get down?" he called, and Vivian sounded quite close as she answered. "If you turn over on your tummy and let your legs down into the hole, your feet ought to touch the top of some steps. I never saw the hole at all till I fell in, but now I'm looking up at the light I can see there were stone stairs there once."

Cautiously Angus did as he was told, and his feet found something solid. Two minutes later he was down in a gloomy place, half cellar, half cavern.

A sudden little bark showed him where Vivian was. She lay between piles of rubble, and snuggled in her arms was Sandy.

"Whatever made you come here?" demanded Angus, as he scrambled over to her. "Are you hurt much? How long have you been here?"

"It's just my leg," Vivian said. "It's all right if I lie still, but it hurts horribly if I try to put my weight on it. I just couldn't climb out and get

Sandy up too."

Angus reached for the sleepy little dog, and sitting up stiffly Vivian told him all about it.

"Grandma's visitors went early," she said, "and I'd been thinking how Betty had taken Sandy for a run on the cliff top. I just wondered if he had liked it so much that he scrambled up the cliff steps while she wasn't looking."

"Jolly good detective work!" exclaimed Angus, admiringly, and he listened to the tale of her search around the tower and the faint yelps she had heard which led her to the tunnel.

"I didn't see any of you about," she explained, "because I came up the track from our lane and not down to the cove at all."

"I'll go and get the others to help rescue you," said Angus, "and Mr Fortescue's probably with them. Susan saw his caravan in the field today." He turned to climb up the rubble and the steps again, and then hesitated and asked, "Weren't you nearly dead with fright, getting down here? I know you're scared of the dark—you told me so."

"You told me something too," answered Vivian. "You told me that if I belonged to God I would never be alone even if I was afraid. Alex told me things too about Jesus being the very best friend. She made me understand that when He died long ago He did it for you and me and everybody, and so I could really trust Him. Soon after that I decided I *wanted* to belong to Him and I prayed and told God I was sorry for all the naughty things I do and asked Him to forgive me. And I know He has. So when I fell down here I asked Him to take care of me, and Sandy too, and I'm sure He sent you to find me."

"So that's why you've been so jolly lately!" cried Angus. "I knew you were different somehow!"

He had scrambled up into the tunnel, when he heard her calling, "Tell them to hurry—I'm so cold and wet. There's water trickling down from somewhere and it's all across the floor where I'm lying."

Angus crawled out of the tunnel and stood up, blinking in the evening light, and as he did so a shadow fell across the path.

Right in front of him stood the tall, red-haired man.

He was about to run when the young man grabbed his collar.

"Wait a minute! Have you been fooling about down there? Don't you know it's dangerous?"

"Let me go!" cried Angus. "One of us has fallen down and she's hurt! I've got to get the others to help—or you must help even if you're a smuggler!"

"Even if I'm a what?" demanded the young man, with a look of blank astonishment, but Angus didn't stop to explain for the sound of voices and running feet told him that the Sandpipers were coming.

He could see Fergus and Donald and Bob, and behind them came striding the tall figure of Mr Fortescue.

"There's Angus!" shouted Penny, as she caught them up, and then she stopped suddenly as the red-haired man turned and she saw his face.

But Mr Fortescue came on, holding out his hand to the stranger with surprise and pleasure. "Vincent Cunningham!" he exclaimed. "Whatever brings you here? What old bones of England's past are you digging up now?"

"The leavings of a Roman garrison, I hope!" answered the young man. "Rumour has it that there's a hoard of Roman coins and artifacts hidden hereabouts, and I've been doing my best to keep my search quiet. I didn't want every holiday-maker and small boy digging wildly and doing damage to the finds!"

The Sandpipers listened wide-eyed, till Angus, remembering Vivian's plight, broke in with his story.

"She's got Sandy! Oh! She's got Sandy!" Betty was beside herself with joy, but Mr Fortescue's concern was for Vivian.

"We must get through this tangle and get her up at once!" he exclaimed, and Angus wondered if they would have to hack down all the brambles, for they could never get an injured girl along the tunnel.

But Vincent Cunningham knew another way out. "There are a whole lot of cellars and tunnels cut in the rock," he explained. "I've been exploring them at weekends for months, and there are some fairly easy steps which come up the other side of the tower, though they're quite hidden by under-growth."

It took them an hour to get Vivian up into the daylight and carry her down the chalk track to the lane.

They took her to the farm first, to get her cleaned up and comfortable, before worrying her grand-parents. Her injury seemed to be just a bad sprain and a lot of bruises.

Angus had raced ahead to give the news, and found his aunt had just returned.

"Wait, wait!" she cried. "Tell me one thing at a time! Smugglers—Roman coins—Mr Fortescue—and Vivians' hurt! Where is the poor child?"

She soon found out. Carefully carried by the two men, Vivian was brought into the farmhouse and all the Sandpipers followed, with Betty and Sandy bringing up the rear.

Mrs Caldwell took things in hand. "Get everybody coffee, Alex," she said and turned her attention to the invalid.

"Why child—you're soaking!" she cried. "However did you get like this?"

"I'm sorry I'm in such a mess," said Vivian, apologetically, "but there was water trickling all through that cellar place."

"There's quite a gush of water coming from somewhere—it must make its way out to sea ..." began Vincent Cunningham and then stopped as he saw the expression on Mrs Caldwell's face.

"Did you say *water*?" she asked faintly. "Did you say a spring?"

"Water!" cried Alex and Penny, hardly believing it. "Why, Daddy can't know about it!"

"It could be piped to the high fields if there's a spring! Oh, Vivian, you've found something wonderful!" exclaimed their mother.

After that their excitement grew. There was so much to tell and so many questions to ask.

Mr Fortescue explained how he had known Vincent Cunningham for years, and how they both had archaeology as their hobby.

The young man told them that he had written

to Mr Caldwell for permission to search for the Roman fort on his land two years previously, but had been prevented from coming by illness. "I didn't write again this time," he said; "perhaps I should have done."

Angus ran up and fetched the two little coins they had picked up by the hide, and both men agreed that they were made in the fourth century.

"I must have dropped those when I lost my compass," said Mr Cunningham. "I used that old war-time lookout on the cliff top as a kind of camp in fine weather. A tent would have made it obvious that somebody was staying around there rather a long time, and I wanted to explore those cellars in peace, and see if I could find traces of Romans lower down."

"But what about the light in the Tower?" cried Penny. "We know Rita really did see it, because Angus heard you talking about it when he wriggled down the Dragon's Chimney!"

Vincent Cunningham laughed. "My young brother came to stay at the cove for the weekend," he explained. "He wanted to discover if the legend was true that there was a cave and tunnel to the tower on the sea side, in a straight line with a light from the topmost battlements. Real smugglers were supposed to have used it in the old days, but we couldn't find it. He hired a boat and rowed out till he could see the light. So much for Rita's nightmare!"

"So that's our mystery solved," said Alex, and then she added, "I do wish Badger had been with us tonight to share in it all!"

"I think you owe a lot to Badger," said her

mother, as she helped Vivian to the couch and tucked a rug over her. "Badger has taught you a lot of things that were not in that wonderful book Angus found in the train. Things about kindness and courage, and trying to learn, and trust in God."

Vivian, clean and warm now, and happy in spite of her aching leg, knew that she too owed a lot to Badger. To Alex as well, and Angus and all the Sandpipers who had helped her to find happiness.

"They will talk about the day I found the water underground," she thought, "but I shall think of it as the day I was certain that Jesus is my friend."

"I guess we're going to owe a lot to Vivian too if Daddy doesn't have to cart water for the cattle next summer," said Alex, almost as if she was reading her thoughts. "She found a buried treasure all right when she fell down that hole!"

"I think she was jolly brave to go looking for Sandy there anyway!" exclaimed Fergus, and those were the sweetest words that Vivian had ever heard. Somebody had called her brave.

"You all seem to have had enough adventures to fill a book since I saw you last!" commented Mr Fortescue, looking round at their eager faces.

Betty, sitting on the hearthrug with Sandy in her arms, said happily, "We'll have an awful lot to tell Mrs Broddie when she gets home from hospital on Monday."

And then she summed up all their thoughts as she added, "Wouldn't it have been dull if Angus hadn't come to live in Catlins Cove!"